Richard Carpenter's

ROBIN OF SHERWOOD

THE HELL MOUTH

Richard Carpenter's
Robin of Sherwood
The Hell Mouth
By John Semper
Published in 2025 by
Chinbeard Books

in association with
Oak Tree Books
oaktreebooks.uk

Original *Robin of Sherwood*
television series copyright ©
1983 HTV/Goldcrest Films & TV.

Editor: Cynthia Friedlob
Sub Editor: Harriet Whitehouse

Adapted from the audio script
The Hell Mouth by John Semper.

Cover art by Robert Hammond,
With thanks to Lucy and Dennis Collin.

The rights of John Semper and Barnaby
Eaton-Jones to be identified as authors of this
work have been asserted in accordance with
the Copyright, Designs and Patents Act of 1988.

Robin of Sherwood licensed, with thanks,
from the Richard Carpenter Estate.

Cover shows Phil Davis as King John,
with Michael Praed as Robin Hood.

Richard Carpenter's

ROBIN OF SHERWOOD

THE HELL MOUTH

by
John Semper

Adapted by
Barnaby Eaton-Jones

A Chinbeard Books / Oak Tree Books Original

INTRODUCTION

by **John Semper**

I was sick with the flu one day in 1984, so I found myself sitting in front of my television in a cold medicine-induced fog, flipping through the channels, searching for something interesting to watch. At that time in my life, I wasn't a habitual TV watcher and had no idea what was on the air in the afternoon. But it was the early days of cable, and there were many more channels to flip through than I had been accustomed to in my lifetime.

Presented with this cornucopia of choices, I landed on *Showtime*, one of the USA cable channels, where I came across something that appeared to be uncommonly well-filmed and extraordinarily well-written. A Jewish man of a bygone era was teaching his children about the Kabbalah. I thought I was seeing a documentary dramatization about Jewish religion and history. I was immediately intrigued, so I continued watching. Imagine my surprise when an opening title soon revealed that the name of the program was *Robin of Sherwood*. I had no idea what any of this had to do with the myth of Robin Hood, but I was hooked. The setting, the music and the costumes were unlike anything I had seen before on television. From that moment on, I became a devout fan of this interesting new series. For the record, the episode I had been watching—as I later found out—was titled *The Children of Israel*.

Fast forward almost forty years later. When Barnaby Eaton-Jones asked me to write an audio drama based on the series, it was a dream come true and the culmination of decades of loving the series. The fact that my story would take place immediately after *The Children of Israel*—the very episode that caught my eye as a viewer back in '84 and had made me a fan of the series—was a wonderful coincidence. It was as if fate had a hand in bringing this incredible project to me.

When Kevin Costner's film *Robin Hood: Prince of Thieves* arrived on the big screen in 1991, it seemed obvious to us *RoS* fans that the Muslim character of Azeem in the movie was most probably heavily inspired by the character of Nasir in our favourite series. Of course, introducing a Muslim character from the Middle East into the Robin Hood saga gave the big-budget Hollywood filmmakers a prime opportunity to cast the very bankable Morgan Freeman, which no doubt added to the box office value of this expensive major motion picture. But it also introduced the concept of bringing a black man to Sherwood Forest. And as I watched that film, I wondered what it would have been like to have brought a black man to the Sherwood Forest of *Robin of Sherwood*. Writing a new audio drama gave me the opportunity to explore that intriguing possibility.

I endeavoured to make my new character's introduction to our cast as organic as possible. In the spirit of the great Richard Carpenter—who was so adept at taking something that was historically accurate and weaving it into the fictional world of *RoS*—my research led me to discover *The Hell Mouth*, the entrance to Hell envisaged as the gaping mouth of a huge monster, which was often featured in medieval plays and theatre. Wrapping a story around the Hell Mouth gave me a chance to indulge in the link between fantasy, mystery and adventure that was a hallmark of Carpenter's masterful writing. Consequently, my black character arrives in Sherwood by way of Italy to help design such a medieval play at the behest of King John.

I won't spoil the plot, but my new character's presence deeply affects one of the main characters in our cast. Speaking of which, it was positively thrilling to revisit all these wonderful *RoS* characters and have them come back to life in my imagination once again.

I do hope you enjoy the story. Barnaby has done a wonderful job adapting my audio play into a very readable novel, and I am honoured to have contributed to the lore of *Robin of Sherwood*, one of the greatest TV series ever produced. As a black writer, I am doubly honoured to have created the first black character that forever will be part of the *RoS* mythos.

John Semper
Burbank, CA, USA
May, 2025

This story is set during series two, directly after *The Children of Israel*.

PROLOGUE

The metallic clang of sword-on-sword echoed around the cavernous hall. A clutch of wax candles wavered in the currents that the flailing weapons were making through the air, sending flickering shadows across the dimly lit space; the flames of a fading fire burned low in the hearth. A weak shaft of moonlight snuck through the opaque greenish glass—a new addition to the bay window on the upper level—and sent a curved spotlight into the middle of the stone floor.

It was in this spotlight that two combatants were fiercely flourishing their swords, blocking and parrying in such a balletic way that it seemed choreographed. Both men were tall and muscular, but seemed unevenly matched.

One sported a bushy blond beard over a chiselled jawline; his stone-cold blue eyes sparkled and his handsome visage was so striking that—even in the half-light—it stood out. His grey chainmail was form-fitting, accentuating a triangular frame with broad shoulders and a chest that tapered away to a smaller waist and long legs. His torso was covered with a white tunic on the front of which a royal herald glinted proudly.

The other was clad in lightweight black armour that reflected the glint of light from the moon. Whereas the bearded man's skin was an unblemished white, there was an odd, dark-green pallor to the other's face as if he were sick, and his eyes were sunken and dark like a deep well that had yielded all its water. His long black hair was greasy and lank, and his lips had a black sheen to them which did not look natural.

'Back, foul demon. *Back*, I say!' shouted the bearded man, both loudly and *very* dramatically.

There was another flurry of sword fighting, ending with the bearded man spinning round on the spot to block an overhead slashing motion by the black-armoured figure. He continued to intone, far too loudly and enunciating each word almost as if it were alien to him.

2

'Though you have the power of evil to lend weight to your sword and strength to your arm, you cannot triumph over the force of good...'

With that, the bearded man suddenly became a whirling dervish of sword stabs and swipes, which the black-armoured man was barely able to block, collapsing to his knees because of the strength of the onslaught.

'And I, King John, fight you on behalf of my subjects with all the power which God, my saviour and my beacon, bestows upon me!' added the bearded man, twisting his sword as it connected with its counterpart, watching it fly from the black-armoured man's grasp. This made the man in black tilt backwards on his knees, both arms melodramatically flung out to either side as he roared in primal rage.

King John went in for the killer blow, 'Die, demon—*DIE!*' he cried. He thrust his sword into the side of his opponent, prompting an unholy scream of blood-curdling agony.

As the demon died—extravagantly—a loud roll of thunder suddenly bounced around the huge hall, sounding like a banging and crashing of drums. A portal at the back of the hall started to open, the frame of which was suddenly alight with blue flames.

King John spun round, his face lit by the increasing intensity of the blue fire which engulfed the portal. 'What is this?' he cried, pointing his sword directly at the portal, 'It can only be the entrance to Hell itself!'

A sonorous voice sounded out from within the fiery portal, echoing and swirling in the confines of the castle's biggest room.

'**King John!**' it cried.

'Hark! A voice calls to me from this maelstrom of fire and brimstone!' said the ruler of England.

'**King John, hear my words.**'

'Who calls my name?'

'**It is I, Lucifer, come to ravage your people and bring turmoil and pestilence to your kingdom.**'

'Lucifer… the Devil!'

'**Yes, the Devil. Yet I go by other names. Some call me the *Horned One*. To others I am *Beelzebub*. Though I am better known amongst *your* subjects as… *Herne the Hunter*.**'

'*Herne the Hunter?*' scoffed King John, 'Why do you appear before me? I've conquered you before, demon. I have cast you out from my lands. I have protected my people. You have no place here.'

'**Just as *your* useless God sent his son to do his bidding, so too do *I* have a son, and his job is to**

4

fight you at every turn, spreading evil throughout your domain.'

'*You* have a *son*? By what name would Herne's evil spawn be known?'

'**His name is *Robin*...**' and there was a pause for dramatic effect, before the voice boomed, '***Robin Longbow!***'

From the back of the hall, a raging voice suddenly rang out; it came from a red face adorned by an unkempt blond beard, and with a gold crown sitting aloft a mop of golden hair.

'*Stop!*' the voice cried, the red face scrunched up in anger, a rodent-like expression plastered across it. 'Stop! Stop! *STOP THIS AT ONCE!*'

CHAPTER ONE

As the command died down, the men in the shadows, who were beating drums for the thunder, paused. The fire round the portal of hell had a bucket of water thrown over it to extinguish its flames. And a waddling, wobbling Master of the Revels came running across the large chamber of the castle, bowing in deference as he did so.

'Is there a problem, Your Majesty?' he asked, as the ornately dressed *actual* King John stood up from his throne and slammed parchment pages down onto the thick wooden table in front of him.

'Yes, there's a problem!' he bellowed, as the fake King John helped the demon in the black armour —who clearly wasn't as dead as he made out—up from the floor.

Why has your actor portraying Lucifer changed the words to my play?'

The Master of the Revels looked wide-eyed and frightened, 'I beg your pardon, sire?' he asked, even though he'd heard what had been shouted.

'Your so-called "thespian" has changed the words *I* had written,' explained the real King. 'The son of Herne is *not* named "Robin Longbow", nor should he *ever* be.'

'No, sire?'

'Of course not, you fool. He is called Robin Hood! *ROBIN HOOD!*'

The Master of the Revels gulped and looked back at his actors, one of whom was hidden behind the no-longer-flaming portal, trying to make himself even more invisible than he'd been when bellowing out Lucifer's lines.

King John picked up the top parchment and waved it at the perplexed face of the Master of the Revels. 'Look at my manuscript. Do you see the words "Robin Longbow" written *anywhere* in my play?'

The Master of the Revels was very used to smoothing over disagreements that were the result of an artistic temperament, and the resultant histrionics and tantrums that came with it. 'I'm sure the players changed it to heighten the dramatic effect, my Liege. A hood is hardly intimidating. But a longbow? Now, *that* is a mighty, death-dealing weapon. It will strike terror into the heart of any audience.'

King John sneered, looking even more rodent-faced. He leant on the table, his small frame pushed forward like a snake ready to bite, as he spat out his incandescent irritation at the man in front of him. 'No one changes the King's words,' he said, furiously. 'When I put quill to parchment to write this play—and when I gave you the position of Master of the Revels—I fully expected you to dramatize my words to the exact letter. If you allow a *single* word to be altered, then perhaps I too shall make changes.' He paused, his sneer turning into a terrifying grin. 'I shall change the position of your head… separating it from the rest of your body.'

The Master of Revels recoiled, clutching at his throat. 'But I— I— I—' he stuttered.

'The peasants have never heard of anyone named "Robin Longbow". That name is *meaningless* to them.'

'A thousand apologies, Your Highness!' said the Master of the Revels, bowing low and backing away. 'I shall chastise the performer at once.'

8

'As well you should! And get rid of that actor playing me; he's too thin! Get someone more muscular and handsome.'

'Um… *more* muscular and handsome?' frowned the Master of the Revels, glancing across to the beautiful and well-built actor currently playing King John, who looked nothing like the real King, neither physically nor facially. How was he going to find someone *even more* good-looking and rippling with *even more* muscle? Yet his tongue spoke out against his brain's resistance, 'As you wish, sire!'

He scuttled off, gesticulating wildly at the actors and the small crew that helped them, panicking that it was *his* head on the block if this play didn't become a cultural masterpiece.

King John slumped back down into his chair and peered round at the fair-haired, stoic soldier who stood to his side. 'Well, Gisburne, what say you?'

Sir Guy of Gisburne, usually stood as deputy to the Sheriff of Nottingham, was enjoying the change of scenery—even if one castle looked pretty much the same as another to him. 'To what, my Liege?' he asked, his deep voice sounding as if it came from of the pit of his stomach, having been marinaded in wine for a few days and allowed to become pickled.

'What say you to what you have seen of my play, you nitwit!' spluttered King John. 'Even though this is purely a rehearsal, you are the only one here seeing it for the first time with fresh eyes. So… what do you think of it?'

Gisburne, used to weighing up his words carefully in his replies to the Sheriff, felt like he needed to do exactly the same with his newly appointed monarch.

'I don't know much about plays,' he admitted, 'I've seen very few. But yours seems to be most entertaining, sire. I'm sure your subjects will enjoy it.'

'Enjoy it? I have no interest in whether or not they enjoy it, Gisburne.'

'No, my Liege?'

'No, I want them to be in awe of it. Better still, I want them to fear it.'

'And what will that accomplish, sire?'

'Good God, man! You're as dim as de Rainault always said. Don't you understand what this play is? It's the Hell Mouth!'

Somewhat smarting from the rebuke, Gisburne almost snapped back, 'The what?'

The Hell Mouth!' shouted King John. 'The most frightening part of the cycle of religious plays performed every Easter. I have given Nottingham the honour of hosting this year's grand Easter celebration. Pageant wagons will gather in the town square; each one will be transformed into an outdoor stage, and each stage will present a religious story... with an exciting new twist. This year, each story will feature an actor playing *me*, involved in some heroic feat. What do you think of *that?*' He grinned, leaning forward, eager for Gisburne's reaction.

'*Every* play will feature you as the hero?' asked Gisburne, hoping his voice didn't register the sheer incredulity that his brain was feeling as he processed what the King had said.

'Yes, *every* play,' repeated the King. 'I might be fending off a French incursion in one. Or, in another, I could be fighting the Turks in the Holy Land. Perhaps I will be—'

Gisburne interrupted, wrongly, 'But you've never fought in the Holy Land, sire.'

'Be quiet, man!' snapped King John, standing up to his full height, which was only impressive because he was standing on a raised platform and Gisburne on the stone floor below it. 'I'm creating a legend; it has nothing to do with reality,' he added.

'My apologies, sire,' Gisburne muttered, trying to stifle a slight smile.

'As I was saying... as per tradition, the final wagon will be a stage built to look like a giant Devil head. And the mouth on the face of the Devil will be depicted as the opening to Hell—thus *The Hell Mouth*. From this gaping maw, an actor will step forth amidst fire and brimstone, dressed as Satan himself. It is the most powerful part of the whole event, the part that strikes fear into the hearts of a gullible crowd. With that fear, I want to accomplish three things. I want the populace to feel like Lucifer has genuinely arrived in their midst. I want them to believe that their beloved Robin Hood is an agent of the Devil. And I want to demonstrate how strong and valiant a fighter I am against him on their behalf.'

'I'm sure your subjects *already* think of you as strong, sire,' Gisburne lied, as if "flattery" was his middle name.

'They do *not!*' snapped King John, 'Word has reached my ear that behind my back, certain rebellious barons—such as Fitzwalter and de Vesci—refer to me as "John Softsword". They think me too weak in my defiance of Prince Philip of France.'

'I have not heard these rumours,' said Gisburne, again employing his ability to lie and flatter at the same time, 'nor do I pay any attention to those that suggest "Softsword" refers to your inability to conceive an heir with Queen Hadwisa.'

King John stepped down off his platform, and stood face-to-chest with Gisburne, looking up Sir Guy's nostrils with a contempt that bordered on the withering.

'What? *What* did you say?' he snarled, threateningly.

'It was… merely a rumour,' Gisburne stuttered, 'and one that I absolutely do not believe.'

King John was fuming and didn't move from his uncomfortably close position in front of Gisburne. 'I've been King barely for long enough to go bed!' he snapped. 'Of all the insolent…' he continued, and then paused, poking his finger directly into Gisburne's sternum. 'I am now regretting pulling you out of Nottingham Castle's dungeon and sending for you when I returned to London. You are beginning to irritate me.'

'My apologies,' muttered Gisburne, who then paused slightly before asking, 'Your Highness… why exactly *did* you send for me?'

'Why, indeed! I thought bringing you back here—away from the Sheriff—might show me your promise. But your promise is clearly broken.'

The King turned on his heel, swinging his robe out behind him, then strode into the moonlit spotlight in the middle of the cavernous space that the actors had occupied. He turned back to shout at Gisburne.

'I want you to escort this troop of actors to Nottingham,' he ordered, 'whilst you also *personally* carry the plans for how I want each of the mansions— those are the stages—to be constructed.'

'I will do my best, sire,' Gisburne replied.

'I'm sure your best won't be anywhere near good enough, though I have had some plans drawn up for you to follow. They are on my table!' he pointed, dramatically, to where he was previously sat.

On the large wooden table, Gisburne spotted a pile of parchments resting. He took the top one from the pile and unfurled it fully to inspect. There was one thing that struck him immediately.

'The texts in these parchments are all written in Italian,' Gisburne said, confused.

'How uncharacteristically astute of you, Gisburne,' shouted King John, striding back towards the table again. He snatched the parchment from Gisburne's hands and proceeded to explain. 'All the best religious presentations these days hail from Italy. The Italians are experiencing a revitalisation and rebirth of dramatic presentation. It began when the Pope banned these kinds of plays from the church. Quite contrary to his intentions, they have taken on a new life in the streets and town squares. A *renaissance*, if you will.'

'Fascinating, I'm sure, sire,' Gisburne said, feeling it was anything but. He couldn't think of anything worse than having to construct a load of stages for the King or having to deal with a bunch of overdramatic actors, tending to every needy whim of theirs.

'That reminds me,' said the King, sitting back down again on the ornate wooden chair behind the table, 'I've sent for an Italian specialist in such productions. He is reputed to be a master of the presentational arts; a genius, some say. It will be his job to design an experience so awe-inspiring that the crowd will be swayed into believing every minute of it is authentic. He should arrive in Nottingham any day now. Tell the Sheriff I want him to extend *every* courtesy to our honoured guest.'

Gisburne was secretly delighted. He wouldn't have to attend the needs of every actor-type. Clearly, the biggest ego of them all would be there as well. And so would this genius Italian specialist. Gisburne inwardly laughed at his own joke at the Sheriff's expense. 'Yes, sire. I shall inform the Sheriff that he—and he alone—must tend to the needs of your visiting genius. How will we know him?' he asked.

'He will present letters of introduction from me that I have sent to him by messenger, bearing my official seal,' explained King John, refolding the parchment and placing it back on the top of the pile.

'I understand.'

King John sneered and chuckled to himself, 'If my play goes as I've planned, the common folk will be convinced that Robin Hood is an agent of the Devil, who visits him in the form of their pagan god, Herne. Hopefully, this will end the people's support of that wretched wolfshead and bring their loyalty back to me. No one in Nottingham will look at Robin Hood the same way ever again.'

As he was speaking, the rotund Master of the Revels came grovelling his way in, and—from a safe distance—informed the King, 'Sire, I think the players are ready for another rehearsal now. We have added more padding to King John's costume, to make him look even more strong, and more rouge to his cheeks to give him a more handsome appearance.'

The Master of the Revels grinned manically, sweat dripping down his brow, and hoped for at least some level of gratitude from the King. He didn't get it.

'Well, don't just stand there, you portly popinjay. *GET ON WITH IT!*'

An owl hooted. Aside from that—and the faint rustling of leaves as a whisper of a breeze disturbed them—Sherwood Forest seemed both still and scary in the dark of night. There was a full moon somewhere above the dark canopy of trees, but it gave out a sickly light and didn't penetrate far into the forest's ceiling.

In the gloom, two figures sat on the lower branches of neighbouring trees; one was short and stocky, the other thin and even shorter. Their silhouettes were only just visible to the well-trodden track on which their eyes were set.

The shorter of the two—with a thatch of auburn hair and such a young, innocent face, that it seemed like he was the unlikeliest of outlaws—was called Much. He was Robin's half-brother, and was still rather naïve in both his thinking and his actions.

'I don't like watching the roads this late at night,' he said, his voice quiet but direct with a peasant's twang to it.

The stockier figure, arms exposed outside of a tunic and a fringe matted onto his forehead, was a handsome-faced man who always seemed to be

17

on the verge of an angry explosion—which showed on his face and in his London-centric voice. Will Scarlet snapped back a reply to Much.

'Why not?'

Much's response belied what strangers might mistake for youthful bravado. 'In Loxley, when I was a boy,' he said, 'there was a storyteller who told us tales of spirits and demons who haunted the forests at night under a full moon.'

Will Scarlet gave out a snort of derision. 'Aww, that's a load of hog-slop meant to scare little kids. There ain't no such thing.'

'Maybe,' said Much, 'but what if those things existed? Look up there. The moon is full. This is the worst time to be out and about.'

'Well, there ain't a lot we can do about it, is there?' sniffed Will Scarlet, adjusting his position on the uncomfortable forked branch. 'Lots of townsfolk are coming from far an' wide for the Easter Pageant in Nottingham, and Robin wants us to mind the roads to make sure they're safe.'

'But who's keeping *us* safe?' whispered Much, his eyes darting about as a sudden stillness—when the breeze dropped momentarily—spooked him.

Will Scarlet ignored the question, too busy explaining their mission yet again. 'He also wants us to keep a lookout for any rich merchants travelling by night; the ones who try to avoid being robbed by us during the day. They never learn! He ain't happy if they sneak through Sherwood without paying us a hefty toll.'

'I *know* that,' Much said. 'I'm just saying why I don't like it here at night.'

'Well, we're stuck here, ain't we? What with us *living* in ruddy Sherwood, an' all.' Will scoffed, not one to be troubled by fear and anxiety.

Much realised he wasn't going to get any sympathy from his companion and changed tack. The mere fact that they were having a conversation was distracting him enough to take his mind off his fear. 'Have you ever been to an Easter Celebration, Will?'

'Not one that wasn't just me drinkin' everyone under the table in Lichfield.'

'Marion told me they put on plays so real they make you shiver. You get to see angels, and even the Devil rise up from Hell!' said Much, drifting off into his imagination.

'Well,' said Will Scarlet, 'if the Devil shows up, he can carry the Sheriff back to Hell with him.'

Much chuckled, 'He'd probably end up sending him back here.'

'Yeah,' said Will Scarlet, 'I can't imagine there's room in Hell for *two* Devils.'

Much began to carry on the conversation, 'Do you think that—'

But he didn't get far, as there was a distant rumbling sound of metal tread on wooden wheels hitting the track, mixed in with the hooves of a horse gently thudding into the ground, which cut across his question. As did Will Scarlet.

'Much! Shhh! I hear something.'

There was a brief pause, as Much and Will Scarlet strained their ears to hear, and the distant sounds became clearer.

Will Scarlet dropped down from his vantage point and beckoned Much to do the same. 'It sounds like a wagon,' he said, as Much landed beside him. 'C'mon,' he urged, and they both crept into the denser foliage near the track on which they'd been spying to get a closer look.

CHAPTER TWO

The wagon that rumbled slowly along the track, its horse seemingly tired and ambling, clearly wasn't in any particular hurry. It wasn't plain and yet it wasn't ornate, and though it had a decoration of sorts, it seemed weathered and faded. It wasn't a type of wagon that either Will Scarlet or Much had seen before now.

'It *is* a wagon, you were right. A big one,' Much whispered, in hushed tones. He peered over the foliage that was blocking his vision to get a better look, only to be yanked back down by Will Scarlet.

'Keep your 'ead down!' he hissed.

'There's only one man driving it,' Much added.

'*That's* odd,' Will Scarlet mulled, seeing the driver a little more clearly as the wagon approached.

'What's odd?' asked Much.

'His face is all covered in a scarf. And it looks like he's wearing a turban.'

'A turbot?' spluttered Much, straining to see this rider with a big flat fish on his head.

'It's sort of like a hat,' Will Scarlet explained.

'Who wears a fish as a sort of a hat?' queried Much, feeling confused.

'What? I never said anything about a fish,' Will Scarlet hissed, himself equally confused.

'Yes you did. You said he was wearing a turbot. We had turbot back at camp once, I remember. Tuck said it was a rare fish to find and an even rarer one to eat.'

'What the..?' spluttered Will Scarlet, 'Much, get your ears washed out. I said "turban", you idiot.'

'What's a turban, then?' Much asked.

Will Scarlet sighed, trapped in their circular conversation. 'It's sort of like a hat.'

Much seemed rather worried about this, oddly more so than when he thought the wagon rider was wearing a large fish on his head. 'We'd better leave him be, hadn't we?' he said, frowning. 'He could be some kind of a sorcerer... or worse.'

'Or... he could be a rich merchant, trying to hide his face so we won't recognize him, and disguising himself under a turban to throw us off.' Will Scarlet surmised, 'Follow me, Much.'

Will Scarlet stood up and began to part the foliage in front of them in order to scramble through.

'Will! Wait!' cried Much, frightened.

'Don't be such a coward. Come on!' Will Scarlet urged, reaching back and grabbing Much roughly by the wrist.

As Will Scarlet and Much appeared on the track through Sherwood, the wagon was near enough to notice them immediately.

'Halt!' cried Will Scarlet, brandishing his sword. 'Just where do ya think you're goin' at this time of night, eh?' he asked, as the wagon came to a stop.

There was silence from the driver.

Sherwood Forest was still. There was neither the hoot of an owl nor the hint of the faint breeze that had played across the leaves when Much and Will Scarlet had begun their lookout duties.

Much tugged at Will Scarlet's faded leather tunic, getting close to his ear. 'He's not saying anything, Will,' he said, worriedly. 'He's not even moving!'

Will Scarlet spoke out again, 'Did you hear what I said?'

Still the silence pervaded the forest.

'Speak, stranger, or I'll run you through with

my sword!' Will threatened, waving it menacingly in front of him.

Suddenly, the silence was shattered by a big, deep, booming laugh from the stranger on the wagon.

It startled the outlaw duo, but Will Scarlet reacted quickly, shouting over it, 'What's so funny? I mean it, I'll kill ya!'

The voice behind the stranger's scarves spoke out in sonorous, rich tones that dripped with an exotic flavour, 'You would threaten to take the life of one who is already dead? Ha! Look... look deep into the eyes of the *morto!*'

The stranger began to unravel the scarves that covered his face, causing Much to stumble backwards a little, and Will Scarlet to intensify his grip on the sword's hilt.

Much cried out in shock, 'His face! It's— it's all black as night!'

The stranger laughed again, throwing back his head as he did so.

'I *knew* it,' Much panicked, 'he's a demon in disguise! I won't look!'

Will Scarlet glanced to the side, at Much. 'Stop covering your eyes, pay attention to—'

But he was cut off, a momentary lapse of attention meaning that he didn't see what came next until it had already blinded him. There was a small explosion. Something had been thrown from the direction of the wagon, and, as it hit the ground near Will's feet, a puff of smoke and a bright, white flash of light caused a commotion in both the outlaws.

The stranger's booming laugh rode roughshod over Will Scarlet's angry protestations. 'Bloody hellfire,' he cried, 'he threw summat at me! I can't see a ruddy thing, Much. *MUCH!* I've been *blinded!*'

Much was too busy whimpering and trying to waft away the wall of blue smoke that had engulfed everything. 'Herne protect us,' he chanted, 'Demon, spare us!'

There was a rustling sound in the nearby bushes, that sounded like a snuffling boar was searching for food, causing Will Scarlet to whip round on his heels. 'Someone's coming up behind me, I can hear them! Much, who *is* it?' he yelled.

Much searched into the smoke, but to no avail. 'I— I don't see *anybody,*' he stammered.

A sharp pain tore into Will Scarlet's leg, causing him to shout out loudly, 'Argh! It's bit me!'

'I saw a dark shape,' blurted out Much. 'It must be an invisible hound from Hell!'

The stranger flicked the reins as he recited some words that neither Will Scarlet or Much could understand, 'Bambola! Bambola del Diavolo! Salire a bordo!' He urged the horse forward with a 'Hee-yah!' and the animal took off at speed, tugging the wagon behind it.

'Watch out!' cried Much, grabbing Will Scarlet's tunic and pulling him sideways with all his strength. Will stumbled and fell in Much's direction, landing heavily on his side and having the wind knocked out of him as he hit the hard ground. The impact released his grip on his sword and it skittered away into the bushes.

'Much, what the hell are you doin'?' he gasped, 'Why'd you pull me over?'

The wagon rumbled on at speed, passing the outlaws and speeding onwards along the track.

'I had to get you out of the way, or the wagon would have run over you,' explained Much, helping Will Scarlet to his feet. 'I didn't think you could see anything?' he asked.

'Nah. But, I think my sight's slowly coming back. You know though, your face looks much better when it's all blurry,' Will Scarlet ribbed, rubbing at his eyes to see if doing so would help give them some clarity.

'Hey!' said Much, in mock outrage.

'C'mon, Much. We've got to get to Robin an' the others.'

'Yes!' replied Much, retrieving Will Scarlet's sword from just off the roadside and taking his arm to guide him. 'We've got to warn them that a demon has come to Sherwood Forest!'

Deeper in Sherwood, the campfire in the outlaw camp was crackling and spitting like it was angry with the darkness that surrounded the circle of light it created and was trying to scare it off. The outlaws, their faces illuminated by the flames, had listened with wide-eyed interest to Much's adrenaline-fuelled story.

'A demon, Much? *Really?*' said Robin, his silky brown hair falling over his shoulders, as he hunched close to the fire. His slim build didn't protect him from cold in the way that Friar Tuck's more ample frame did, though his several layers of clothing were useful for keeping out the nighttime chill.

'We saw him with our own eyes,' said Much. 'His skin was black as night. His eyes glowed like embers in the campfire. And he had fangs that dripped blood.'

'You saw this too, Will?' Robin asked.

'Yeah,' said Will Scarlet, his vision virtually back to normal and his eyes now looking less bloodshot, though they were still sensitive enough that he needed to sit a little further back from the flickering flames. 'Well, no. Not all of that. I saw his skin; the rest might've been summat Much made up. He made me blind for a bit.'

'Much made you blind?' asked Friar Tuck, confused.

'No, the demon did!' answered Much.

The imposing figure of Little John—bedecked in a warm furry tunic, and with his unkempt beard accentuating his jutting jaw—stood nearby, leaning against a tree trunk. He ran a hand through his hair as he spoke, 'How'd the demon make you blind, Will?'

'With a bright light. It flashed white in my face, John.'

'He cast a spell, he did,' interjected an over-excited Much, 'and then he conjured up a demon hound from Hell! He called it a Bambola! That's what he said. "Bambola"! Honest!'

'Will?' queried Robin.

'Yeah, that is exactly what he said.' Will Scarlet confirmed.

'Are you sure?' asked Robin.

'He didn't blind me in the ears,' came the grunted retort.

'And you two are certain you didn't drink any bad ale while you were out?' asked Marion, her pretty elfin features breaking into a grin, framed by her frizzy auburn hair. She knew Will's propensity to have a "quick one" at any inn—or any village— he passed on his travels.

'We didn't touch a drop, I swear,' Much said, earnestly.

'Did you eat any bad mushrooms? You know, the ones that cause you to see things that aren't really there?' asked Friar Tuck, recalling an incident from the past far too well.

Will Scarlet, famously hot-headed, was starting to get irritated by the line of questioning, especially when they'd encountered and defeated worse things that had seemed just as magical or strange. 'I know you won't believe this, Tuck, but not everything revolves around food.'

Friar Tuck smiled. 'Fair enough, Will. You've made your point.'

'Not quite,' said Will, 'the dog—'

'Hell hound,' corrected Much.

'—well, whatever it was... it bit me on the leg.'

Will Scarlet stood up, and presented one leg towards the fire light, showcasing a darkening patch of blood on the ripped fabric, through which could be seen a nasty wound.

Marion leapt up, always the first to offer aid when a situation arose in which her supervision and knowledge might be needed, especially in the treatment of cuts, bruises and wounds. 'Will, let me help stop the bleeding.'

'I'll survive,' came the muttered reply.

'Not if I don't look at it first. It needs the blood stemmed. Now, sit down and let me tend to it before it goes bad.'

'Marion, I said I'll survive. Don't make a big fuss over it.'

'Sit!' ordered Marion, knowing the way to handle Will was to be more confident than he was angry. He muttered something unintelligible under his breath as Marion moved him closer to the fire, to see what she was dealing with. She ripped more of the fabric away and began to apply pressure with a clutch of leaves she'd scooped up before reaching him.

'Ow!' smarted Will Scarlet.

Marion ignored him, but was studying the wound as she dabbed it. 'These don't look like any bitemarks I've ever seen. They're more like tiny stab wounds.'

'—from the teeth of a demon hound from Hell!' reiterated Much, who was fidgeting about on the floor, sitting cross-legged.

'I pity any hellhound that took a bite out of your flesh, Will Scarlett. He's bound to be drunk for weeks,' joked Friar Tuck. Will Scarlet's reply was nothing other than a deathly stare supposed to frighten Tuck, but which only made him chuckle.

Little John—still standing impassively on the rim of the light that shone from the fire—was troubled. 'What do you think, Robin? If a demon is loose in the forest—'

'—then he probably wouldn't be driving a small, horse-drawn wagon with just his dog for company,' Robin said, finishing Little John's sentence. 'Perhaps we should see if we can catch up with this mysterious creature and find out what—or whom—he really is,' he added and turned his head quickly sideways to call out a name. 'Nasir!'

The previously-silent Saracen stepped out of the shadows from which he had been listening and observing. 'Yes, Robin?' he asked.

'You, John and I will make our way to the road to see if we can find this demon,' Robin ordered.

Yet before anyone could reply or even draw a single sword, a rich voice called out to them.

'Why bother, when the demon has come to find *you!*'

The closest to the interloper, Nasir was also the first to react, unsheathing a curved sword and instantly holding it under his cloth-covered chin.

'Nasir, wait! Don't cut his throat; he's unarmed!' Robin shouted, standing up.

Much scrabbled backwards to be the other side of the fire from the stranger who had so silently crept into their camp. 'That's him,' he whimpered, 'that's the demon! Herne protect us! He's come to steal our souls!'

'Quiet, Much,' barked Robin, before turning to Marion's impatient patient. 'Will, is this the man you encountered?' he asked.

'That's 'im!' exclaimed Will Scarlet through gritted teeth as Marion attended to his leg wound. 'Even though his face is covered, I recognise that voice.'

'And his turbot!' exclaimed Much.

'*Turban,*' Will Scarlet growled.

'That too,' Much agreed.

'Who *are* you?' asked Robin.

'I am but a humble traveller.'

'And what do you want with us?'

'Perhaps some food and a mug of ale to warm my blood on a cold night?'

Little John moved from where he was stood, walking over to be closer to the intruder. 'It's hard to offer generosity to a man who hides his face,' he said. 'Remove your scarf; let us see what you look like.'

'Fine... if this man here will take the point of his sword away from my neck?' he asked, indicating Nasir before throwing in a sarcastic jibe. 'I am positive he is a clumsy bungler when it comes to handling a sword, and I don't want him to hurt himself trying to cut my throat.'

Nasir grimaced and held the sword where it was, 'You take a bold chance, stranger.'

'I'm sure you were a stranger once, too.'

'Withdraw your sword, Nasir!' ordered Robin.

Nasir grunted and reluctantly did as he was told. 'As you wish, Robin.'

'Thank you.' said the visitor. 'Now, do not be afraid. I'm not making any sudden moves. Allow me to remove my scarf and show you my face.'

As his face was exposed, Much gasped audibly,

even though he'd seen it once before. 'Look!' he cried, 'I *told* you his skin was black as night! He is a demon, indeed. Herne, protect us!'

Friar Tuck patted Much—whose initial backwards crawl had placed him at the feet of the man of the cloth—on the shoulder. 'There, there, Much,' he said, soothingly. 'Be still. This is no demon; he's as human as we are.'

The stranger looked directly at Nasir. 'Does this black face bring any recognition to your memory, Nasir Malik Kemal Inal Ibrahim Shams ad-Dualla Wattab ibn Mahmud?'

Nasir was stunned. 'Alonzo?' he asked, his normally expressionless face breaking into a grin that totally transformed his features. *'Alonzo?* Alonzo da Pian del Carpine?'

The stranger nodded and grinned in return, 'Embrace me, my good friend, for I have come a long, long way to find you!'

Much couldn't quite believe what he was seeing. 'Nasir! You can't hug him! He's a *demon!*'

Rather than correcting Much for a second time, Friar Tuck blurted out, 'By all that's Holy... he can say Nasir's full name!'

Little John smirked, 'None of *us* can do that,' he said. 'This is no demon; he's a bloody *genius!*'

CHAPTER THREE

It was impossible to tell whether it was day or night in the Great Hall of Nottingham Castle, as the candles and the fire in the hearth seemed to be lit almost permanently. The full moon outside did not permeate the inside of the magnificent stone structure, though it made no difference, anyway. If the Sheriff was up and demanding food or wine, *everyone* was up to attend his needs. As he entertained his brother, the Abbot, the kitchen was still busy preparing the final course.

Sir Guy of Gisburne had returned from London and had made a decent attempt at explaining what King John's plans were.

The Sheriff's eyes narrowed to a squint, and he raised his eyebrows as he reacted to Gisburne's long-winded account of the Royal court. 'The Hell Mouth, you say?' he asked, enunciating every word in a clipped tone that made each sentence spoken sound as though it had been carved out with extreme care.

'Yes, my lord Sheriff,' said Gisburne, almost feeling glad to be back. If the Sheriff's sarcasm and tantrums had seemed bad, they'd paled into insignificance when matched up against those of King John. 'You've heard of it?' he questioned.

'Of *course* I have, Gisburne. Unlike you, my brother and I were given a robust education in the religious arts.'

The Abbot raised his wine goblet, which the Sheriff assumed was in appreciation of his jibe against Gisburne, but—in a split second—he turned it upside down and the Sheriff realised he was indicating that he'd run dry.

Woman, bring us over more wine!' shouted the Sheriff to the servant who was stood near the small table strewn with food and drink nearby, as she awaited her orders.

'Yes, m'lord,' she said, 'right away!'

She brought a jug to the Sheriff's table, her lined face creased with stress and worry as she never had become used to being shouted at. She accidentally sploshed the tiniest drop of wine on the table, as she attempted to steady the jug over the Abbot's receptacle.

'Don't pour it, you tired old twig!' snapped the Sheriff, 'Just leave it and get your wretched wrinkled face out of my sight!'

'Yes, m'lord Sheriff!' she mumbled, then backed away as quickly as she'd arrived to stand behind the other table and make sure she was out of the Sheriff's line of view.

The abbot, pouring the wine, decided to pontificate. *'The Hell Mouth,* Gisburne, is the culmination of the religious plays we in the Church once mounted every Easter. It's the most terrifying part of the cycle…'

'So I've been told, Abbot Hugo,' agreed Gisburne.

'Yes. Terrifying,' interrupted the Sheriff, '*if* you happen to be a simpering three-year-old child!' He drained his wine from the goblet and put it down so clumsily on the table that it nearly fell off the edge, before continuing 'So, our king wants to be the hero of a childish fairy tale? And he thinks that will turn the public against Robin Hood, does he?'

'That is his plan,' Gisburne replied, matter-of-factly.

'Then he is a bigger fool than I thought. And for the sake of this ridiculous play, he has undertaken to pay for our entire pageant instead of letting it fall to the purses of the trade guilds as is customary?'

'So it would seem.' Gisburne nodded.

'Well, we must let him. And we must make sure to receive our fair share of the royal purse in the form of a sizeable entertainment tax. Right, Hugo?'

Abbot Hugo glossed over his brother's greed and added his own thoughts to the matter. 'I have no idea why the Pope expelled such a popular ritual from the Church. As a proud Abbot servicing my flock, I looked forward to the large crowds of the faithful it brought in every Easter.'

'Yes,' said the Sheriff, rubbing his hands together, 'and the hefty tithes that accumulated in your coffers.'

'Robert, must you always be so *vulgar?*'

'I only speak the truth, brother. Our father raised us to be practical above all else.'

'And *you* grow more like that heathen every day.' Abbot Hugo muttered, clearly more of a mummy's boy himself.

'Gisburne,' barked the Sheriff, 'I trust you had no problem escorting the performers here to Nottingham?'

'None, my Lord.'

'And you've shown them to their quarters?'

'In the stables, yes.'

Abbot Hugo, aghast at the revelation of their location, almost choked on his wine. 'You've put the actors in the stables, Robert?' he spluttered.

'Of course, brother!' snapped back the Sheriff, assuming that the Abbot was soft on these travelling show-offs.

But that wasn't the case.

'You spoil them!' sneered the Abbot, 'It's far better than they deserve. When they performed for the church, we made them camp outside on the grounds near the pigs.'

'Rightly so, Hugo. It is an odious profession,' chuckled the Sheriff, 'but these are the King's actors, so I had to make slightly better accommodations— for appearance's sake if nothing else. I do hope the horses will forgive me.'

Back in Sherwood, Robin was quizzing their new arrival as the fire burned low.

'How did you find us, Alonzo?'

The rich timbre of Alonzo's voice washed over the outlaws in an almost hypnotising way as he explained, 'The legend of Robin Hood—the people's hero of Sherwood Forest—has travelled far and wide. I was living in Italy when I first heard of you. You are all quite famous. You, the portly Friar Tuck, the tall one named Little John, the beautiful maiden Marion.'

Much bent forward now, 'What about me?' he asked eagerly. 'Am I famous?'

'Yes. You're a famous pain in the backside!' laughed Little John, his eyes twinkling in the firelight.

Alonzo continued without answering Much, 'When I heard of a deadly Saracen who wielded two swords and was nigh-on invincible, I knew it had to be my old comrade in arms.'

'You fought with Nasir?' Will Scarlet asked, looking at Nasir, who nodded sagely.

'Side by side, Will Scarlet,' said Alonzo, 'during many a bloody campaign in the Holy Land. I've tolerated his companionship, even though he is a clumsy bungler when it comes to handling a sword.' He laughed heartily, clearly insistent on ribbing his good friend's proficiency with his blades and taking his ego down a notch or two.

'We've saved each other's lives many times,' Nasir added, quietly.

Alonzo took a long swig of his drink, smacking his lips afterwards and wiping his sleeve across his mouth. 'This ale is good!' he exclaimed, 'I was chilled to the bone.'

Little John was intrigued by something, which he assumed everyone else was thinking but perhaps were too polite—or too afraid—to say. 'How did you find our camp?' he asked.

Alonzo smiled, 'It wasn't very hard. After my encounter with your two men, I found somewhere to hide my wagon, then doubled back on foot and followed them both here.'

Will Scarlet bristled. 'But that's impossible. I didn't hear a thing.'

'That is my speciality,' Alonzo smiled.

'How did you blind me?' asked Will, suspicious of this stranger still.

'I ignited a dash of a certain powder with a small flame. No more than a magician's trick.'

'What kind of powder?' asked Little John.

'A rare acquisition from my travels in foreign lands.'

'So… you came all this way just to see Nasir?' Little John queried.

'No, I wish I could say I had,' Alonzo said as he looked over at Nasir. 'Sorry, my friend.'

Nasir nodded again, showing his understanding.

'I am on a mission,' continued Alonzo. 'I have come to see your Sheriff.'

'The Sheriff of Nottingham?' gasped Much.

'Unless there is another Sheriff around here?' Alonzo gently mocked. 'I'm afraid I have business with him.'

Will Scarlet snorted, with disgust, 'Hah! He's hardly a tolerant recipient of strangers. He won't be anxious to do business with a foreigner.'

'Unfortunately, he will have to,' said Alonzo, producing something from his deep pocket. 'You see, I come bearing the seal of the King.'

There was a tangible change of mood in all of the outlaws, almost like they were preparing to attack. It was palpable, and Alonzo was very well aware of it.

'Emissary from King John, eh?' rumbled Little John, standing straighter.

'I am, indeed,' said Alonzo, raising up a passive palm to gesture compliance, 'But calm yourselves. I have no need to inform either him or the Sheriff of your whereabouts.'

Robin had got up from where he sat, and was illuminated a pasty orange by the remaining flames trying their best to raise themselves higher from the fire. He asked, 'So why are you here?'

Alonzo grinned. 'For the Easter revelries! I no longer pursue the ways of the warrior. I am a performer, a conjuror... an actor! My wagon is my stage.'

The outlaws relaxed a little.

'I have come to mount a production for the King as part of the Easter celebration. It will be one of what the townsfolk call the Mystery Plays!' Alonzo added.

'How does a warrior come to be an actor?' asked Little John, one hand on his hip and the other stroking his beard thoughtfully. He wasn't ready to believe everything that came out of Alonzo's mouth.

'We're all performers on this stage of ours we call "life." And we are not always whom we appear to be,' Alonzo mysteriously intoned, his eyes fixed on Little John almost hypnotically.

'Aye, and that's what we're afraid of,' said Little John, 'that you are not what you appear to be.'

Alonzo broke his gaze and grinned again, 'There's no need to be alarmed, John Little. I have come to perform on behalf of the King. Your adventures are not my concern. I came to you only to see an old comrade-in-arms. Sit. Please. Let us enjoy our libations in the spirit of friendship! And then, I will be on my way. I give you all my word.'

Little John put his hand on Nasir's shoulder, as Robin spoke, 'Nasir, is the man's word to be trusted?'

'I swear upon my sword.'

'But you have two!' laughed Alonzo. 'Surely you'd better swear upon them both!'

This broke the tension, and as Nasir smiled, Little John relaxed enough to walk back and sit by the fire as Alonzo had requested.

'I swear upon both swords,' a smirking Nasir stated.

'In that case,' said Robin, patting the log next to him on which he was sitting, 'you are welcome to enjoy our hospitality for as long as you need.'

Alonzo sat down, flapping his robe out behind him so he didn't sit directly on it. 'Thank you, Robin Hood.'

Much, who had now scuttled away from Friar Tuck's legs and closer to the warmth of the fire, looked earnestly at Alonzo. 'May I ask you something?'

'Of course,' Alonzo said, quietly, returning Much's gaze.

'Where is your dog?' he asked.

Alonzo frowned, puzzled by the question. 'Dog?' he queried, 'Why, Much, I have no dog.'

CHAPTER FOUR

The night had moved on, the clouds had partially covered the full moon, and the fire was alight again now Little John had fetched some more logs. The sounds of any nocturnal woodland wildlife were drowned out by the revelry around the flames. Food and drink were being consumed, stories were being told, and—in Nasir and Alonzo's case, sat aside from the rest of the group and indulging in their own conversation—memories were being shared.

Alonzo's laughter was almost like a rumble of thunder crossed with a wheezing bellows, as he tried to get to the end of his sentence. It showed the black humour and fearlessness of warriors, that this particular memory was something he felt he could laugh about.

'…and what about that night we were set upon by thieves in Constantinople?'

Nasir smiled, 'We were outnumbered, ten men against the two of us.'

'I think it was more like twenty, my friend!' boomed Alonzo. 'Such a shame. I have always felt guilty that the odds were so heavily in our favour.'

'How long did it take to slay them?' asked Nasir, matter-of-factly.

Alonzo quietened his voice, a poetic quality in his words causing a lull in his good humour, 'Only the time it takes for a bead of hot wax to run down the side of a lit candle.' Then, he grinned from ear to ear, 'And we still had enough energy to make love to the barmaids in the tavern nearby. Those were good days.'

'They were.' Nasir agreed.

Alonzo seemed suddenly saddened. 'We were once soldiers who fought for noble causes!' he intoned. 'Now look at us!' He pointed at Nasir. 'You are a thief hiding in the forest,' then pointing back to himself, 'and I am a harlequin, eager to dance like a hop-frog for any person willing to pay me handsomely enough.'

'Not every crusade comes with a shield and banner bearing a sigil,' Nasir almost whispered, as if he was afraid that this was the most he had spoken in his whole time of being with the outlaws. His grasp of English was always improving, but he preferred to be a man of action rather than a man of words.

'Not every crusade, no. However, the ones they sing about in ballads do!' Alonzo laughed, but then his voice too dropped to almost a whisper. 'And yet, my song is almost over now.'

Nasir leant closer towards Alonzo, 'What do you mean?' he asked.

'The thing is, Nasir… I am dying.'

Nasir was stunned. 'Dying?' he muttered, a frown suddenly etched into his forehead.

'I am stricken with an illness; it's in my gut. You can't see it, but I ache in pain and I bleed in ways that are unnatural.'

'I am sorry.'

'I can tell my days are finito, Nasir. As a warrior, I had hoped to go out at the end of a worthy opponent's sword. Alas, Allah makes plans without our consent.'

'Your place in Allah's realm is assured. You have always fought as his loyal servant.'

'Yes. But I would still prefer to fight one last good fight for one last good cause. It is my prayer that Allah will allow me to do so.'

Off to the other side of the camp, the others spoke quietly to Robin.

'Look at the two of 'em over there. They've been talking like that for hours,' Will Scarlet grumbled, though truth be told he was itching to hear what was being said, due to the laughter from both Alonzo and Nasir that permeated the air.

'I don't think I've ever seen Nasir talk this much across all the time we've known him,' said a surprised Marion.

'Aye,' said Little John, 'and I've never seen Nasir let another man call him a "clumsy bungler" once and live to utter it again, let alone twice. I wonder what they're talking about?'

'Old friends reminiscing about the past,' smiled Friar Tuck, biting on a piece of half-cooked meat and trying to chew it.

Much had been studying Alonzo the entire time, watching him like a hawk from across the campsite. 'Robin? Why isn't his skin the same colour as ours?' he asked.

'His ancestors come from a different land, Much,' Robin explained, 'a land where everybody's skin is the same as his. Some call it Kush. Others call it Nubia. In our country, he's called a "Moor".'

Surprised, Friar Tuck stopped his chewing and

looked at Robin. 'And how do you know so much about foreign lands, Robin?'

Robin smiled and looked up from under his fringe at Tuck. 'As Herne's son, I have learned much from the visions he presents to me. I have seen lands far away from here as well as the people who inhabit them. I have learned much about their histories, their customs and even their languages.'

Much wasn't finished, and was as inquisitive as ever. 'But Alonzo… is he different from us?'

'His customs may be different,' said Robin, 'but deep down, he's exactly the same as us. He eats, sleeps, loves, laughs and cries just as we do. He shares our likes, our dislikes and our strengths.'

'Yeah, and our weaknesses, Robin,' interjected Will Scarlet. 'Do you really believe that a fighter like him is only here to put on a play?'

'I don't know what to believe or disbelieve, Will. But, if Nasir vouches for him when he says he's not here to cause us harm, then I won't worry about that… for now, at least.'

In the courtyard at Nottingham Castle, lit by the waxy moonlight, a rider on horseback seemed to appear from almost out of nowhere and, pulling on the reins, skittered to a halt on the cobblestones. The half-asleep guard on duty jumped to attention.

'Halt!' he cried, rather redundantly. 'Who goes there?'

The rider, dressed in the finest burnt orange, pulled back on a hooded cloak that complimented his outfit to reveal a ruddy-cheeked oval face, adorned with a fine brown beard speckled with grey... yet not a follicle of hair grew elsewhere on his head. His nose was lopsided from his time spent in tournaments, and he had the bearing of someone who had little patience for those he believed were beneath him.

'I am Eustace de Vesci, Lord of Alnwick Castle,' he proclaimed, 'I am here to see the Sheriff of Nottingham.'

The guard, knowing a noble when he saw one, ushered him in.

Striding into the Great Hall of Nottingham Castle, having first been led to the stables to deposit his horse before being ushered through the kitchens to reach the Sheriff, the nobleman's presence wasn't unexpected; the guard had summoned servants to inform Robert de Rainault of the man's arrival.

The Sheriff, standing in front of the huge table that sat on a platform at the back of the hall, opened his arms wide and began to walk towards the approaching, imposing figure. 'De Vesci!' he cried.

The Lord of Alnwick Castle nodded and grasped one of the Sheriff's outstretched hands with both of his, pumping it in a handshake that was more a show of dominance than a friendly greeting. 'De Rainault!' he echoed, speaking the Sheriff's name.

'Well, this is an unexpected surprise.' The Sheriff beckoned to the plush seats near to the roaring fire. Beside them was placed a small stand on which a pre-prepared jug of wine, two goblets and a silver platter of assorted meats (surrounded by thickly-sliced carrot pieces coated in honey) could be found. The servants had been nothing if not hasty in sorting the food out before the Sheriff's visitor had made it from the stables to the vastness of the Great Hall. 'Come, warm yourself,' beckoned the Sheriff. 'Dine and drink with me!'

The bald visitor, throwing off his cloak as the heat from the fire became too much, plonked himself down on one of the chairs. 'Very kind; I shall.'

'Woman!' barked the Sheriff, and from the shadows of the hall came a plainly-attired servant, with hair scraped-back into a bun and a grovelling, shuffling walk.

'Yes, my Lord Sheriff?'

'Bring us wine!' he shouted, theatrically swiping the jug from the table and watching as it shattered in the burning hearth, the sizzling red liquid causing the flames to sputter ferociously as they deposited a sweet, sickly smell in the air.

'That... *was* wine, my Lord Sheriff,' the servant stammered.

'You call that wine? That was hog swill. I could smell it from here. Or is that *you* I can smell? Either way, only the very best is to be served for my guest.'

'Ummm... yes, sire...'

'And be quick about it, you old hag!'

'Yes, my lord. Of course, my lord.'

As she scuttled from the chamber to head for the cellar where the Sheriff stored the best wine, the Sheriff sat himself down too, and reached for a glazed carrot which he popped into his mouth and chewed whilst speaking, 'What brings the Lord of Alnwick such a long way to my doorstep on a cold night like this?' he asked, 'And at such a late hour?'

De Vesci spoke in an urgent, hushed whisper. 'There are plans afoot, my dear Sheriff, and I wanted to make sure you stayed on the best side of them.'

'*Plans?*' repeated the Sheriff, 'What plans?'

'Assassination.'

The Sheriff was shocked by the blunt reply. 'What? Of whom?'

'I speak of nothing less than the assassination of King John himself.'

The Sheriff sat back and squinted in suspicion at the visiting nobleman. 'Have you gone mad, de Vesci?' he sneered.

'No, far from it. Hear me out.'

'I will... before I throw you out!' warned the Sheriff. 'This had better be good.'

'Even in the short while since Prince John became King John, there has been incessant talk of him yielding too much land to Philip of France. The northern barons have had enough. Robert Fitzwalter has organized a rebellious faction, of which I am a member. But, if we can achieve our goal *without* civil war, then all the better.'

The Sheriff's hooded eyes had widened considerably during the explanation, 'Good God, man!' he spat out, both in panic and in rage. 'You speak not only of murder but of treason. Just having such a conversation could see us both hanged. Why have you brought this insanity to my doorstep?'

'Because,' said the murderous plotter, 'we have chosen the date and location for where we want the deed done.'

'Have you now?'

'We have.'

'And let me guess where that might be…'

'It is right here. In Nottingham.'

'Yes, I suspected as much.'

'When King John comes to attend the Easter pageant and partake of the Mystery plays, his life is to be snuffed out. To have this happen, we need *your* help.'

There was an incredulous pause from the Sheriff, who let a piece of meat he'd picked up just hang in the air. 'Why on earth would I help you with this outrageous plan?' he asked, biting the meat in two angrily, like a vulture picking at a carcass.

'The Barons will pay you well. And *you* risk nothing. All you must do is stay out of the way. I'm sure you can handle that, can't you?' De Vesci had reached deep into his tunic and retrieved a large leather purse, which he threw on to the little stand. The clatter of the landing, on the side of the silver platter, produced the familiar chink of gold coins, and the Sheriff snatched it up to pull open the tied top. De Vesci smirked, as he saw the Sheriff's face light up—both metaphorically and literally—as the gold coins became exposed to the firelight and shone bright. 'This is merely a downpayment,' he said, 'You'll receive triple what is here when the deed is done.'

'Indeed,' sighed the Sheriff, eyeing the gold greedily, 'that *is* a hefty sum.'

There was a pause as the Sheriff weighed up his options, much like he was weighing up how much gold the purse contained. 'You *do* have my interest,' he confirmed.

'Good.'

'But what do you mean by "stay out of the way"?' the Sheriff asked.

'We'll need for you to find a plausible reason to withdraw yours and the King's soldiers at the appointed moment, so that the King is left unprotected. And...' De Vesci left the sentence hanging in the air, like a bad smell.

'*And?*' queried the Sheriff, finally.

'My soldiers will be in disguise and ready to attack.'

The Sheriff snorted, derisively, 'You're a fool to think common soldiers can be relied upon for so delicate a task. What if they bungle it?'

'We've anticipated that. We have hired an assassin to come here and handle the job cleanly and professionally if all else fails.'

'An assassin, eh? Who might this assassin be?'

'He might be any one of a number of people, my dear Sheriff. It is best if his identity remains a secret for now. I can say that he is a foreigner. He will arrive in the guise of someone who is here to participate in the Easter plays. That is all you need to know.'

'Soldiers in disguise? A foreign assassin? All of this will seem conveniently planned. Why won't suspicion immediately fall on you barons... or, for that matter, on me?' asked the Sheriff.

'We were hoping you could help us with that, as it's the perfect, ready-made alibi. Blame the assassination on the notorious outlaw Robin Hood!'

'Blame it on the wolfshead? Ha!' The Sheriff chuckled, contemplating the situation. 'As outrageous as your plan is, perhaps you have managed to convince me. If it rids me of Robin Hood, and turns the people against him, what have I to lose?'

'None of this will fall on you, Robert. Should this plan go wrong, all blame will be on *me*. You will be innocent of any involvement.'

'You are damned right about that. I will make sure I will be absolved of any complicity. And if they cut off your head, I will be the one in the crowd cheering the loudest. However, until then, it appears you and I have a bargain.'

De Vesci grinned, exposing a worrying lack of teeth. 'Then, if that be the case, let us drink to it!'

The Sheriff went to pick up the jug that was no longer there, and then remembered he'd flung it into the fire in a temper. 'Where is that stupid woman with the wine?' he whined, before shouting, 'Bring me that wine, *now!*'

Another servant popped his head into the Great Hall, afraid to step fully inside. 'She is on the way, my Lord Sheriff,' he said, a tremble running through his voice.

The Sheriff held the empty goblet in his hand and plastered a smile on his face that looked more duplicitous than pleasing, as he narrowed his eyes and looked at the beads of sweat running down the bald head of the nobleman that sat opposite him.

'I wish to drink to the death of Robin Hood!' he said.

CHAPTER FIVE

Alonzo's wagon rolled speedily along the Sherwood track, its decorative sides suddenly appearing more alive as the early morning shafts of sun hit them. It had been a fairly short journey to the edge of the forest, where Nottingham Castle came into view. Upon seeing it in the distance, the accompanying Robin and his band of outlaws, all on horseback, came to a jittery standstill.

'Thank you for allowing me to spend the night at your camp, Robin,' Alonzo said.

'My pleasure.'

'And for escorting me through Sherwood this morning to the Sheriff's castle.'

'As beautiful as Sherwood is, it can still be dangerous for a sole traveller. But now, this is where we must leave you. The Sheriff and I aren't exactly on speaking terms.'

I understand. Arrivederci, Robin Hood. Peace be unto you.'

'And to you, Alonzo.'

Alonzo turned to the other side of the wagon, where the silent Saracen rode. 'My friend, Nasir. It has been wonderful to see you again.'

Nasir nodded, in appreciation, 'It too has filled my heart with joy.'

'Much!' shouted Alonzo, and Much tumbled off the back of Marion's horse and strode up to hold on to the side of the painted wagon. 'When we build the stages for the pageant, you are invited to come visit and see what we've done.'

'Oh, I'd like that!' Much excitedly cried, 'Thank you!'

Alonzo turned back to Nasir again, 'Nasir! *Assalamu alaykum,* my brother in arms.'

'*Wa alaykum as-salam,*' Nasir replied.

Alonzo gently whipped the reins, and the horse started to pull the wagon forward to Nottingham Castle. 'Farewell to you all!'

It wasn't long before Alonzo was out of earshot; Little John climbed down from his horse, intending to walk it back to camp and spare it from his bulky frame in the saddle. 'Now, how d'ya suppose the Sheriff is going to react when he catches sight of *him?*' he laughed.

'I'm sure the Sheriff will roll out the grand welcome that he gives to all strangers,' replied Friar Tuck. 'You know, the one where he instantly assumes the worst and throws them into the dungeon.'

'I think you're right, Tuck.'

'Then he will be shocked when he learns Alonzo was sent by the King himself,' Nasir stated, trying not to show how worried he was about his old comrade.

Robin turned his horse round, and headed back towards their camp, 'I'd give anything to be a fly on the wall when Alonzo arrives at the castle.'

The Nottingham Castle gatehouse was manned by a sentry who wasn't quite as half-asleep as the one before him who had let in the Lord of Alnwick. As a gaudy but grainy wagon approached, slowly dragged by a tired-looking horse, the guard shouted, 'Halt! Who goes there?'

'I am here to see the Sheriff of Nottingham!'

shouted back Alonzo, the reverberating timbre in his voice resonating across the space left between sentry and wagon.

'Are you *mad*, you foolish Moor?' sneered the sentry. 'The Sheriff won't even think of consorting with the likes of your black kind.'

Alonzo, well used to the level of abuse to which his appearance exposed him, ignored the ignorant swipe. 'I come under the authority of King John,' he stated, knowing full well what response he would receive.

As anticipated, the sentry laughed with no attempt to disguise the scorn he felt for the driver. He walked closer to the wagon. 'Hah,' he snorted, 'that's a good one! And I order you to get lost under the authority of my arse. Now, sod off, or I'll run you through with my sword.'

The sentry drew his sword from its sheath, and the blade glinted in the morning sun.

'Well, if that's the way you want do this…' sighed Alonzo, drawing his sword and leaping down off the wagon, '…you are welcome to try!'

'Why, you arrogant fool!' exploded the sentry, and thrust his sword at Alonzo's chest, who deftly parried and instantly pushed the soldier sideways. Before he could even regain his balance, Alonzo had swung round and deftly kicked his feet out completely from under him, and he crashed—face forward—into the hard, stone ground with a clatter that ricocheted off the castle walls.

Alonzo turned the guard over with his foot and stood above him. 'Now, my friend, while you're grovelling there in the dirt, are you going to fetch the sheriff or not?'

There was a determined look on the sentry's face. He knew his duty and he was going to stick to it, even if it meant dying to do so. 'To arms!' he shouted, as loudly as he could between gasps of air, 'To arms! Raise the alarm!'

It was mere seconds before the heavy patter of feet turned into the sight of more soldiers, coming to the sentry's rescue.

'Stop the Moor, stop him!' cried the sentry, from the floor.

Alonzo grinned. 'Ah, more sport,' he chuckled and ran at the five approaching soldiers, swirling his sword above him like a man possessed. This alarmed the soldiers who had expected him to retreat, and the momentary confusion allowed Alonzo to crash into two of them at the forefront, flinging them over. The remaining three were hardly able to register what was happening before Alonzo had swung his sword across them, causing each to block his blow instinctively. The soldier at the rear stumbled backwards and considered running in the same direction to reach the safety of the castle.

Sir Guy of Gisburne, his shock of blond hair bouncing as he ran, then skidded to a halt outside the gate, sword already in hand. 'What is going on here?' he yelled.

The soldier who had thoughts about retreating yelled back, 'We are under attack by this Moor!'

'One black man is able to hold off every single one of you?' bristled Gisburne.

Alonzo had spotted the new interloper and shouted whilst blocking and parrying, 'Indeed, my sword is barely tickled by their meagre efforts!'

The jibe incensed Gisburne, who could just about hold his temper with the Sheriff, but often let out all his pent-up frustration from having to do that on everyone else he met.

'Stand clear, men,' he ordered, 'and let *me* handle this!'

The soldiers didn't need to be asked twice and scrambled to get out of the way of the Moor's whirling dervish of an attack.

Gisburne's attacks didn't seem to make any meaningful difference to the situation, even though his red face showed the immense exertion and power he was putting into the swordfight. 'Hah!' snorted Alonzo, *'You're* in charge here, are you? I am *not* impressed.'

From a safe vantage point on the castle's ramparts—having wondered what was going on outside—the Sheriff's voice could be heard, even though he hadn't shown himself for fear of being a target. 'What *is* all this commotion?'

The rearmost soldier—who had now fully fallen back—shouted up to his employer, 'There's a Moor trying to enter the castle, sire. He claims to be sent by the King! But I believe Sir Guy will soon kill the impudent fool!'

There was a brief pause where all that could be heard was Alonzo's rich laugh and Gisburne's enraged grunts of effort and anger over a backdrop of metal-on-metal as their swords clashed and re-clashed in quick succession.

'A *Moor?'* the Sheriff suddenly shouted, in a mild panic, *'Stop!* Tell Gisburne to stop!' He didn't wait for the soldier to do so, and just yelled, even louder, *'GISBURNE! STOP!'*

Gisburne pulled away his sword and danced backwards, not showing the relief he experienced in walking away from a duel in which he felt like his opponent was not only letting him play, but also even sparing his life.

'*Stop?*' laughed Alonzo, 'What a shame; I was just getting warmed up.'

The Sheriff peered over the battlements—carefully—and caught sight of the impressive Moor. 'Who are you?' he cried, 'What business do you have here?'

Alonzo bowed, and in doing so rubbed his aching stomach. He might still have had the speed and agility, but whatever was ailing him increased in pain when he partook in such feats of physicality. He straightened up again, pushing the pain to the back of his mind. 'Allow me to introduce myself,' he said, sheathing his sword, 'I am Alonzo da Pian del Carpine. I have been sent here by King John. He requested I venture here from Italy to preside over your Mystery Plays this Easter.'

Gisburne, exhausted and leaning heavily on his sword, grumbled loudly. 'You? *You* are the Italian specialist?'

'At your service,' Alonzo grinned.

The Sheriff, from up on high, as usual singled out his deputy. 'Gisburne, you idiot! This man is our guest, and he is to be treated as such… not skewered by the tip of your sword.'

Gisburne stayed silent, as the Sheriff then ignored him and focused on the sword-fighting victor. 'Greetings, Signor Alonzo!' he intoned, 'I am Robert de Rainault, the Sheriff of Nottingham. My apologies for this less-than-ideal welcome. Please forgive the idiotic impertinence of my soldiers, and allow me to offer you the hospitality of my castle.'

'Why, thank you, my lord, though no apology is necessary. I like a good sword fight in the morning; it gets the blood flowing through my veins.'

'Gisburne, have our guest's horse and wagon properly tended to.'

Gisburne snorted, 'You expect *me* to wait on *him*?'

'I do,' replied the Sheriff, 'Unless you want to spend the night in the dungeon for insubordination.'

Gisburne sulkily walked over to the Moor's wagon and horse, taking the reins and pulling gently. 'As you wish, sire,' he muttered.

'Come, Signor!' said the Sheriff to Alonzo below, 'Please allow my soldier to escort you to your rooms. I shall be down to greet you properly in one moment. We rarely receive foreign visitors in Nottingham.'

'That may have something to do with your unique form of hospitality,' replied Alonzo, ever ready to display his sarcastic wit.

The Sheriff disappeared from view and made his way to ground level, whilst the soldier nearest the gate gestured to Alonzo, who took the hint. He walked into Nottingham Castle with Gisburne following behind, leading his horse and wagon like a servant.

the Sheriff disappeared from view and made his way to ground level while the soldier mounted the gate returned to stand by who took the clay he walked into alleyway in Castle with his arm following behind finding his knees understood like a coward

CHAPTER SIX

Moving through Sherwood Forest as quietly as they could, the outlaws were on a hunt… though not for food, but for a woman.

'I'm sure I saw her headed this way, Robin,' Much said.

'What would an old woman be doing wandering alone in Sherwood?' queried Will Scarlet, always ready to assume that anything or anyone they came across was a potential trap.

In the middle distance, a plainly dressed lady was steadily but doggedly making her way through the thick undergrowth.

'Look! Do you see her, Robin? There!' pointed out Much,

'Yes, Much. I see her.'

Little John chimed in, 'Perhaps she's lost?'

'No,' said Robin, 'She's walking with purpose; she's looking for somebody.'

Marion, who had been peering over Robin's shoulder, suddenly pulled him to an abrupt stop. 'Just a moment,' she said, 'I *know* her! Her name is Agatha; she's one of the servants in the Sheriff's castle. She was always nice to me when I lived there. Maybe she's in trouble?'

Marion overtook Robin and dashed off into the undergrowth.

'Marion, wait!' cried Robin, fearful—much like Will Scarlet—of this being some kind of set-up to catch him or others from his band of outlaws.

'Agatha!' shouted Marion, as she crushed bracken and fern underfoot.

The servant woman stopped in her tracks and turned to see Marion, leaping over the uneven forest terrain like a balletic gazelle to reach her.

'Lady Marion!' exclaimed Agatha, breathing a huge sigh of relief, 'Thank God I've found you at last!'

'Why are you here?' Marion asked, urgently.

I have something important to tell Robin Hood, and it's a matter of life or death. Can you find him for me?'

Robin seemed to step out of the forest magically, which had appeared to be a wall of green until the dashing young man with the long brown hair emerged. 'I am here. What is it you need to tell me?' he asked.

Agatha was somewhat taken aback by the sudden realisation that Robin Hood was stood in front of her within seconds of her asking to speak with him. She couldn't help but stare at the outlaw, a little open-mouthed, taking in his lithe form— his slashed-to-the-waist shirt, his tunic, skin-tight trousers and faded leather boots. He was as good-looking as the tales about him told, but he also possessed a calm presence that felt both strong and stoic yet also gentle and caring.

'I'm sorry,' said Robin, 'did I startle you?'

'Yes,' Agatha admitted, still in a bit of a daze.

'Then please let me introduce you to my friends, so you aren't shocked by them too.'

As Robin introduced them by name, Little John, Will Scarlet, Friar Tuck and Much all came out of the foliage and stood behind Robin. Agatha was even more amazed.

'You needed to tell me something?' Robin asked again.

Marion gently nudged Agatha, who closed her

mouth and suddenly remembered why she was there. 'The King!' she cried. 'They're plotting to kill him!'

'Who is?' asked Marion, gently.

'A man came to the castle very late last night to visit the Sheriff. A nobleman with an odd-sounding name, he was one of the barons of the north. I think he was from… er… I want to say Candlewick..? Candlewick Castle..?'

Robin's mind whirred, 'I think I know who you mean.' he said, taking Agatha's trembling hand, 'Was it Eustace de Vesci, Lord of *Alnwick* Castle?'

'Yes, that was his name,' smiled Agatha, suddenly feeling less fearful.

'I know of him,' said Robin, 'Please, continue.'

What Agatha said next did in fact shock Robin and the outlaws just as much as Agatha had been by their appearance in front of her.

'The barons are sending an assassin to kill the King when he visits Nottingham for the Easter celebrations,' Agatha blurted out.

'Are you *sure,* lass?' urged Little John.

'Yes.'

'Assassinate the King?' thundered Little John. 'Have they gone *mad?*'

Will Scarlet's permanently suspicious streak got

the better of him, as he hissed, rather threateningly, 'How do you—a *servant*—know all this?'

'The sheriff treats servants like me as if we are invisible, y'see. Like we are stupid. Thus, his tongue is loose and he speaks freely of things a wiser man would choose to keep secret. He asked me to fetch him more wine, but I waited just outside the Great Hall, to listen to what they were saying.'

'You deliberately listened in on his conversation?' sniffed Friar Tuck.

'I did,' admitted Agatha proudly, 'Had I not gone to fetch wine, I would have been stood in the Great Hall anyway. I'd have heard because he believes we are insignificant, and that spouting secrets in front of women matters not... but women have minds and hearts; we are strong and principled. I *knew* there was something secret being planned, and I wanted to find out what—in case it might affect us!'

'That's just as deceitful as the Sheriff, though,' Little John said, disapprovingly.

Marion disagreed, 'Not so, John. If the Sheriff is stupid enough to treat women with contempt— and, believe me, I know from experience he is— then he deserves neither privacy nor loyalty.'

'I am loyal to the *crown*,' stated Agatha, 'as are all of the castle's servants. I will not stand back and see the King murdered when I can do something to prevent it.'

'Agatha, who is the assassin that the barons have hired to kill the King?' asked Robin.

'I know not his name, I'm sorry. All I know is that he is from another land.'

'A foreigner?' added Friar Tuck.

'Yes, that's right. And, once the deed is done, the Sheriff intends to blame it all on you and your friends here.'

'Why, that weasly little runt...' grunted Will Scarlet through gritted teeth.

Robin gently patted Agatha's hand, both for reassurance and to mark the end of the conversation. 'Thank you, Agatha, for bringing this news to us,' he said, then turned to Much behind him. 'Much, you go with Marion to escort Agatha back to the castle. Be careful nobody sees you.'

'Of course, Robin!' said Much, eager to help.

Marion took Agatha's hand and began to lead her away, 'Come with us, Agatha,' she said, walking back along the trail the servant girl had made.

As they left, the rest of the outlaws heard Agatha proudly making the point, 'We women are not *quite* as invisible as they believe us to be, are we, Lady Marion?'

They could just about hear Marion, chuckling and replying, 'No, we certainly are not, Agatha.'

As they both laughed almost conspiratorially, Much walked ahead, leading the way through the forest and back to Nottingham Castle.

Little John was first of the remaining group to speak when Marion, Much and Agatha had vanished into Sherwood. Looming over Robin, he asked worriedly, 'What do you make of it, Robin?'

'It's an outlandish plan,' admitted Robin, 'but I believe her.'

'Who do you think this assassin might be?' asked Friar Tuck.

'All we have to go on is that he'll be a foreigner. Yet the answer, it seems, might be all too obvious.' Robin paused and then looked across at the Saracen in their midst. 'Nasir?'

'Yes, Robin?' replied Nasir, his face betraying the fact that he knew what he would be asked.

'Your friend, Alonzo—what was his speciality when you fought together in the Holy Land?'

'He was an assassin. The very best.'

'I suspected so. He was able to track you, Will, without you spotting him. That took a lot of skill.'

'Do you think we need to keep an eye on him, Robin?' Little John asked.

'Hard to do that without arousing his suspicions.' Nasir said, knowing his friend and speaking for Robin.

'Nasir's right—' Robin confirmed, though he was interrupted before he could finish.

'Then what are we gonna do?' Will snapped.

'There is *one* man who could do it,' declared Robin.

'And who's that?' asked Little John.

'Much.'

'*Much?*' coughed Will.

'Yes, Will,' said Robin, grinning. 'Don't you remember, Alonzo invited him to come visit whilst he built his "mansions"—his stage wagons. I'll have Much take him up on that promise. Perhaps we can discover Alonzo's true purpose here before King John even comes close to Nottingham.'

CHAPTER SEVEN

Time often passed lazily in Sherwood, but the fortnight that had gone by had seen a flurry of activity. In a small clearing, flattened and groomed to accommodate the King's Easter Pageant, the sounds of hammering and construction were still drowning out the peace and quiet of the countryside.

Alonzo, standing out among the rest of the workers—not because of the colour of his skin but because of his bearing and his height—had been tailed by Much for many of the days that he had been working diligently with everyone to build something that would amaze the Nottingham populace.

'Hand me more of those nails, Much!' he ordered, with a hammer in one hand; in the other was a piece of particularly stubborn wood that wouldn't stay where he needed it to.

'Yes, Signor Alonzo,' Much said, scrabbling for the nails that were needed and passing a handful over.

Alonzo sighed, but with a smile. 'Please, Much, I have told you a thousand times: just call me "Alonzo", I am fine with that.'

Much protested, grinning in his boyish way, 'But I *like* saying "Signor"! I've never had a chance to speak a foreign language. And I've never met *anyone* like you before.'

'You mean, a man with black skin?' Alonzo asked, seemingly throwing the question away into the wind as if it were the hundredth time he'd had to ask it.

'No,' said Much, 'I mean an artist like you. I have never seen anybody paint the things you can paint. Or build what you can build. Over these last... well, over the many days I've been by your side, I have seen you make such beautiful things.'

Alonzo stopped what he was doing and leant back to rest on the wooden frame. He seemed genuinely touched, especially from one so young who had yet to form his own opinions about people and places. 'Thank you, my friend,' he said, before continuing in a ruminative way. 'It's funny. As a soldier, I often bore witness to ugliness. I never knew I had any appreciation for beauty left in me until I started doing this. Come Easter night, this whole clearing will be filled with people and firelight and stage wagons full of colour and majesty.'

'Do you miss being a soldier?' asked Much, innocently.

'Soldier, no. *Warrior...* perhaps.'

'Robin says a battle is only as good as the cause worth fighting for.'

'Robin's a very perceptive fellow, Much,' Alonzo said, then quickly changed the topic as if he didn't want to delve too deeply into more violent days gone by. 'But enough about that. Help me carry some of my painted backdrops. Come, follow me.'

Issuing his polite order, Alonzo strode towards the structure to which he had been trying to fix the wood. Much hung back, suddenly hesitant.

'But... I— I—'

'What's the matter?'

Much attempted to form a sentence for a second time, 'I don't... I don't know if... no, I can't...'

Alonzo suddenly realised he was stood under the giant archway, 'Ah! You're afraid to walk through the Devil's Mouth. Is that it?'

Much nodded, solemnly. 'I think it might be bad luck.'

'My boy,' smiled Alonzo, 'it's just a giant wood carving of the head of the Devil. A huge prop. A stage illusion.'

'But... well... you've made him look so frightening,' Much explained, not looking directly at the structure, nor the opening where Alonzo stood that represented its mouth.

Alonzo walked back towards Much, 'That's the idea!' he said. 'All this paint, all of these props and set pieces... they're all designed to create an illusion—to make the audience believe everything is real. But it is all just a magic trick. *That* is what theatre is all about.'

Much threw a tentative glance at the giant head, and—in the light of day—the joins and nails and jagged edges showcased the work of the construction rather than the shadows and grooves of a real face.

'On the night of the play,' explained Alonzo, 'when the actor dressed as Satan passes through this giant Devil's head of a doorway, all watching will be convinced that the *real* Devil walks among them. It is a vision they will never forget.'

Much looked both worried and a little confused. 'It won't be a real Devil, will it?'

Alonzo let forth one of his booming laughs, which seemed to come from the pit of his stomach. 'I assure you, my dear Much, it most definitely will not be...' And then he cried out in pain, he clutched at his midriff, and his knees buckled, as he staggered to the Devil's Head to lean on to something before he fell.

'Signor Alonzo! What's wrong?' asked a panicked Much urgently, rushing to his side and no longer afraid of the wooden head to which he was now close.

Alonzo's face was twisted in silent agony; his groans and grunts pushed back down his own throat with a force of habit as he tried to control the pain. 'Boy...' he grimaced, in anguish, '...Fetch me... my... medicine!' He took a deep breath, held it a few seconds, and then let it come rushing out alongside the words he needed to say. 'It's in a green bottle in the back of my wagon. Quickly. Hurry!' he urged.

Much ran to Alonzo's wagon at full pelt, nearly crashing into its side. He scurried around the back and pulled aside the curtains that kept the interior dark, cool and mysterious. Inside, it was like a combination of an apothecary's stall and a toymaker's workshop. Peering in, Much scrabbled around, desperate to find the bottle Alonzo had requested.

'Green bottle. Green bottle. Where *are* you, green bottle?' He soon spotted it, nestling a little further back in the wagon. 'There you are!'

Much went to reach for it, but jumped as he saw two small figures of the Devil behind where the bottle was stood, as though somehow it was being guarded by them. Their legs were splayed out, their arms hung limply by the sides of their torsos, and their heads stared forwards, though were cocked slightly to one side.

'Oh, no!' he muttered, slowly reaching in for the green bottle. 'Herne protect me,' he pleaded as his fingers reached round the bottle's base. As he pulled it gently towards him, he glanced up at the Devil dolls, each roughly the size of a human toddler. Crying out in terror, he clutched the bottle as hard as he could and raced away from the wagon, back to Alonzo.

Alonzo, clearly struggling to stay upright, grabbed the bottle from Much's grasp. 'Good; you found it!' he puffed out between rasping breaths. Pulling the stopper from the top, he drew it clumsily to his lips and, tipping his head back, drank quickly and heavily.

At first Alonzo gasped from both the speed at which he had drunk the liquid and the pain that had overcome him. But once the liquid had reached his stomach, Alonzo quickly felt better. Desperate to show appreciation to his young saviour he said, 'Thank you, Much. My pain… it now subsides.' But his eyes then caught sight of Much's face and it instantly bothered him.

'I'm sorry, did I frighten you? I am better now, I promise.'

Much shook his head, 'No, it wasn't you.'

'Then, what was it, boy?' Alonzo asked, concerned at Much's white pallor. 'You look like you've seen a ghost.'

'Not a ghost, no… but… you know those Devil dolls in the back of your wagon?'

'Ah, yes,' nodded Alonzo, 'The marionette figures. What about them?'

'I was looking at the face of one of them when I took the bottle…' Much trailed off, shivering with shock.

'Yes, they were specifically made in order to frighten the—'

Much interrupted him, 'His eyes moved!'

Alonzo chuckled, not strong enough to regain his booming laugh, but with enough force to irritate Much. 'No, lad, no. That didn't happen.'

'I swear, I saw it!' said Much, earnestly.

'You imagined it! You got *the fear*,' explained Alonzo. 'Those marionettes were sculpted by a genius named Benvenuto Cellini; he made them as a special favour to me. His unparalleled artistic brilliance is what infuses them with life.'

'But—' Much began.

'It was all in your mind, boy. All in your mind,' soothed Alonzo, feeling a little more like his old self now the pain had returned to the dull ache he was more used to.

'What are they for? Why do you have them?' asked Much.

'They're part of the grand finale of *The Hell Mouth*. I'm planning a *big* surprise for the audience... especially for King John. It's a surprise he'll never forget!'

CHAPTER EIGHT

Nightfall in Sherwood was both a beautiful and haunting time. Much didn't like it, particularly after his experience in Alonzo's wagon; he was happy he'd made it back to the reassuring glow of the campfire before dusk had truly left the day behind and the night had blanketed the sky above.

He had already told the others what had happened earlier in the day, in between picking at the bowl of fish stew that Friar Tuck had presented him with. 'And that's what he said: *There will be a big surprise at the end, especially for King John,*' Much explained.

Marion, who was sat next to him and engaged in tying her auburn hair into a plait, looked over at Robin. 'That certainly sounds ominous,' she said.

Robin nodded. 'It does, indeed.' He got up and patted Much on the back. 'You did well, Much. Thank you.' He then walked over to where Nasir was stood, at the outer rim of the camp as lookout for any accidental or purposeful interlopers. 'Nasir,' he said, 'you know Alonzo best. What do you make of this?'

Nasir was uncharacteristically chatty for once, not just dishing out short sentences and one-word answers. 'He told me he would like to die as a warrior. If the barons convinced him that killing King John was a cause worth fighting for, then, yes, he could well be the assassin.' Nasir paused, looking intently at Robin in order to convey the gravity of his next comment. 'Alonzo would make a most formidable foe, should you try and stop him.'

Robin wasn't sure if it was a warning or a threat but hoped it was the former. 'And yet, try we must,' he said, walking back to sit at the fire again. 'Come the night of the Mystery Plays, we must be on our guard to protect the King. As much as we dislike King John, it won't go well for us if we allow him to be assassinated in Nottingham.'

As he sat down, he saw that Nasir had gone from the camp. 'Nasir!' he shouted, 'Where have you gone? Nasir!'

Much, who had seen Nasir walk out of the light of the fire and into the forest's gloom, got up and ran after him, shouting loudly, 'Oi! Nasir! Wait for me!'

Robin began to rise in order to follow Much, but Marion gently pulled him back down by the hem of his oversized shirt. 'Robin,' she said, calmly, 'leave Nasir for now. He just wants to be alone. He'll be annoyed enough that Much has gone after him. He has a lot to be concerned about when it comes to Alonzo.'

'As do I,' Robin replied, more curtly than he intended. Marion frowned.

'What do you mean?' she asked.

'Nasir only agreed to join our fight after the death of his master, the Baron de Belleme—as you'll well remember. But this is not his home. And he has fought with us only for a short time.'

'Surely you don't question his loyalty?' Marion queried.

'I haven't… up until now,' sighed Robin, 'but when it comes to a choice between loyalty to you and me versus loyalty to an old friend and comrade-in-arms from his past, I honestly have to admit, I don't know if we have yet done enough to earn his trust fully.'

Little John, sitting on the other side of the fire and peering over the flames had been stroking his beard thoughtfully throughout Robin and Marion's exchange, having himself held back from getting up and going after Nasir too.

'With all the respect I can muster, Robin,' said Little John, 'that's absolute nonsense.'

Robin bristled but Marion put a gentle hand on his thigh, trying to help him stay calm.

Little John continued on, proving that he wasn't criticising Robin at all; quite the opposite, in fact. 'You've certainly done enough to show him beyond a shadow of a doubt that you—and all of us—are against tyranny, and that you're all about making the lives of the peasants in Nottingham better than they have previously been under the Sheriff's wicked rule. That's all he has *ever* needed to know to trust you. That's all *any* of us ever needed to know.'

Marion decided to add her own thoughts to this, keeping her hand placatingly on Robin's thigh, 'A few weeks ago, you were doubting Will's loyalty before we rescued the de Talmont family… but your fears were proven to be unfounded. Now, you're concerned about Nasir. Robin, you have done more than enough to prove to him and all of us that you are the right one to be our leader.'

'*Have* I?' worried Robin, who was suffering from a momentary crisis of confidence.

The young rebel, barely in his twenties and bristling with the injustice people received purely because of where they were born, had become somewhat of a legend across the land. The pressure of being known so well—in addition to his work keeping his friends safe, the villages around Sherwood fed, and the times he stood toe-to-toe with the Sheriff and Gisburne when each new tax or tithe or plan reared its head—was immense. And that wasn't even counting the mysterious forces of evil the outlaws had battled that were beyond Robin's control or reasoning, and, like Herne, seemed to come from an alternative realm. It was a great deal of weight for his shoulders to carry and sometimes, inwardly, he felt as though he were stumbling, or taking the wrong fork in the track.

'When it comes down to Nasir making a choice between Alonzo or me, can we bet our lives on him choosing me?' he asked. 'What if Nasir chooses Alonzo? Will that make him *our* enemy, too?'

Later that same evening, back in his usual spot at the very edge of the light that emitted from the fire, Nasir sat sharpening his blades. The scraping noise echoed into the forest, but didn't seem to disturb the rest of the snoozing or supping outlaws, who were closer to the fire's warmth. Much had been sat watching Nasir at work, fascinated by his precision and the fact that he spent more time than his colleagues did in taking care of his weapons, always managing to refine his swords to be sharper than any other. Admittedly, Robin's sword Albion never seemed to require any attention, but Much knew it contained the magic of the forest and of those who claimed it beforehand. But Nasir's swords were crafted in a foreign land and were kept razor-sharp purely by Nasir's constant attention.

Nasir held his second sword up and looked over at Much. 'There. What do you think, Much?'

'It looks so very sharp!' exclaimed Much.

'It is sharp enough to cut through bone,' Nasir stated, matter-of-factly.

'Nasir, may I ask you a question?' asked the inquisitive youngster, who looked incredibly fresh-faced compared to the rest of them.

'Ask.'

'Alonzo is your friend…'

'Yes.'

'Could you really kill him?'

'Why do you ask such a thing?' Nasir queried, a small frown crossing his swarthy features.

'It's just that… I've gotten to know him, from spending so many days with him lately. At first, I thought he was nothing like us… but now…'

'Now you see beyond his black face. You see a man like us. A man of honour.'

'That's right! He seems like a good man, Nasir. And… and… I *like* him!'

'I, too, have great affection for Alonzo. Much, we each choose our own path though, and we must suffer the consequences of where that path leads. As a man of honour, Alonzo would be the first to understand that.'

There was a slight pause, as Much was ruminating. He then said, with a note of worry in his voice, 'Robin says we have to stop Alonzo if he tries to kill the King. But I hope Robin's wrong about him. I'd hate to see Alonzo die.'

Nasir nodded, putting away his swords as he explained the code by which he and Alonzo had lived for years. 'For men who are warriors like us, there is no greater gift than to die an honourable death. That is the truth for Alonzo, and for me…'

'What about Robin?' asked Much.

'Yes. Even Robin.'

It was the night of the Easter celebration, and the sounds of music and revelry washed over the highly-populated clearing where Alonzo and the rest of the troupe had been working so diligently for the last few weeks.

The stages were set, the audience were full of anticipation, and the beautiful glow of a horde of candles bathed the angled structures and expectant faces in a warm glow. There was magic in the air, even though it was a fool's magic, where theatrical artifice would combine with the villagers' imaginations, and create a spectacle both memorable and believable.

Nearby, Robert de Rainault, the Lord High Sheriff of Nottingham, sat straight-backed and proud on his horse as he approached the Easter offering, his short height disguised by his bearing and his mount. Next to him, on a shining white steed, was the equally diminutive figure of King John, his straggly beard and wavy dark-blond hair teased by the breeze. Both men were similar not only in stature, but also in their vanity and selfishness; both possessed a quick temper and sarcastic tongue.

Riding slightly behind them on a muscular black mare with the wildest eyes was Sir Guy of Gisburne. He was security and protection to King and Sheriff on their short journey from Nottingham Castle to this man-made clearing on the outskirts of Sherwood Forest. He was taller than both men in front of him, but often slumped in the saddle when with his superiors—not just in deference but also because he knew how narcissistic noblemen could be... and there were only so many poisonous verbal barbs he could endure.

King John marvelled as he scanned the masses who had come from villages far and wide to see what delights were on offer at this free festival and threw out an off-hand congratulation to the Sheriff. 'This turnout exceeds my wildest expectations, De Rainault,' he grinned, excitedly.

The Sheriff agreed, deferring back to the King, 'When word circulated that none other than King John would be attending tonight's Easter festivities, loyal subjects travelled many miles in order to see you.'

'Nothing to do with us threatening to burn down their villages if they *didn't* attend, was it?'

Gisburne muttered under his breath, smirking to himself and wishing he had the courage to join in the conversation and actually deliver the line to the men he was guarding.

The small group were virtually on top of the clearing now, and people had spotted their arrival.

'What was that, Sir Guy? I didn't hear you with all this noise,' King John asked, turning his head slightly to direct his question behind him.

Gisburne spoke up louder, 'I said that all the villages burned with a passion to see their King, my liege.'

King John smiled, proudly, 'Tonight they shall see me aplenty. I will be engaged in feats of daring and bravery, thanks to these plays and the fine actor portraying me.'

'Absolutely, Your Highness!' fawned the Sheriff, 'They will appreciate your love for them as never before.'

The three horsemen entered the clearing and tried to direct their horses through the crowds.

'Make way, you stupid fools!' shouted the King.

'Yes, make way for your gracious, caring King!' added the Sheriff, loudly.

CHAPTER NINE

From a vantage point on the outskirts of the Easter celebration, hidden amongst the trees that surrounded the clearing, Robin and the outlaws were surveying the scene and staying out of sight… for now.

'What do you make of it, Will?' asked Robin.

Will Scarlet, who had been scanning the area diligently for the past five minutes, replied, 'Looks to me like there's a fair few soldiers in disguise an' hiding their swords. I counted at least thirteen of 'em. And none of 'em look familiar.'

'Hmmm. They are likely De Vesci's men,' said Robin, turning to his trusted, tall, bearded deputy. 'What about you, John?'

'Aye, I agree with Will,' said Little John, cradling his wooden quarterstaff in his fist, in readiness to use it should he need to. 'At least thirteen, maybe even more. All scattered throughout the crowd.'

Marion chimed in, 'They do seem to be concentrated mostly near the final wagon, *The Hell Mouth*—Alonzo's stage.'

'Then that is where they plan to make their move,' said Robin, keeping a watchful eye on the proceedings. 'We'll have to position ourselves near there to hold off any attack on King John.'

Friar Tuck, ever the pragmatist, threw a difficult question into the conversation. 'How can we hope to defend the King against De Vesci's men, the Sheriff's men *and* the Moor assassin at the same time?'

'We will surround the King,' explained Robin. 'He's the one they want. If we can spirit him away quickly into the forest, we stand a chance of keeping him alive. Much, where is Alonzo?'

'He is in his wagon, getting ready for his play.'

'Marion?' said Robin, turning to her.

'Yes, Robin?'

'Find some horses for us and ready them behind Alonzo's wagon. We may need to make a fast exit.'

Marion nodded a silent reply.

Robin turned again, his attention now focused on his Saracen brother. 'Nasir, you must keep an eye on Alonzo.'

'I shall,' Nasir promised, his black leather outfit allowing him blend well into the shadows and the darkness of night.

Robin sighed heavily and then smiled. 'Time to put on our own performance,' he said. 'Places, everybody! Spread out... but surround that Hell Mouth. And may Herne be with us.'

The outlaws dispersed like startled deer, though Much hung back to talk to the always-ambling Friar Tuck. 'Tuck, can I ask you something?' he asked.

'Of course you can, Much. Anything.'

'Seeing Alonzo put together his play got me to thinking...'

'There's a first time for everything,' said Friar Tuck, but Much didn't even hear the joke, so intent was he on his query.

'Is there *really* a Devil? Is there *really* a Hell?' he whispered, almost afeared that the underworld would hear should he speak too loudly.

Friar Tuck smiled, placatingly, and delivered a small lecture that he knew might one day come in handy as Herne became the deity that the outlaws believed in. 'That, young Much, is a matter of faith, and everybody should be free to believe what they choose to believe,' he began. 'But, truth be told, none of us knows for sure if either exists—'

'Oh,' Much said, not expecting that answer.

Friar Tuck hadn't finished though.

'—but what we do know for sure is that there is "evil", and that there are those who are willing to do evil things to get what they want. And when they try, there'll always be good people like us who will do our best to stop them. If we do the right thing, and stand up for what is good and just, then all we'll ever see of the Devil is his backside as he flees, returning to Hell where he belongs and where we don't.'

'Right,' Much said, the thoughts in his head cascading like a river in spring that chased and twisted at speed, threatening to overflow and flood the area. Friar Tuck's explanation had built the riverbank higher and contained the churning waterfall of questions, such had been its clarity and wisdom on what Much thought would be an impossible subject to explain. He looked at Friar Tuck's gentle, soft face, with the serious determination of youth. 'Tonight,' he said to Tuck, 'we'll stop someone from doing something evil.'

Friar Tuck put his arm around Much's shoulders. 'That we will, my boy. That we will.'

The atmosphere in the clearing was one of excitement. Even though many of the villagers had been forced to leave their homes to gather for the plays, once such a throng congregated, they couldn't help but be intrigued and full of excitable nattering.

In the ornate box, on a small platform that had been constructed for the Royal visitor and his entourage, Abbot Hugo had been sat waiting for the arrival of his brother the Sheriff, along with the newly-crowned King. As it had been positioned in such a way, the box had the best view of all the stages at once. The stages themselves were in a semi-circular arch and the crowds stood in rows in front and to the sides of the Royal box.

Well, Hugo?' said the Sheriff, noting the almost permanently sour look on his brother's face, who often looked like he'd swallowed something rotten. 'How do you find the view?' he asked.

Abbot Hugo sat up from his slumped position and adjusted the expensive rings that decorated his purple-gloved fingers. He gave an answer the Sheriff wasn't expecting, which was less than flattering.

'We are sitting out in the open in a crudely-constructed platform on hard wooden seats looking at stage wagons cobbled together by common rabble,' he began, with his dour, nasal whine audible to the Sheriff—though, fortunately, not to the King. 'When my Church put on these Easter plays, our mansions were much more elaborate… as were our accommodations. This is pathetic.'

The Sheriff, refusing to be broken by Hugo's damp spirit, smiled widely and kept his good humour. 'Oh, I don't know, Hugo; I think this is all rather grand. The Moor has done an especially fine job building the Hell Mouth.'

Abbot Hugo grunted with disdain, not wanting to admit that the spectacle of a large Devil's Head— with a mouth wide open and hollow eyes that seemed to be lit from within—was anything other than ordinary, and poured more scorn on proceedings. 'But these wooden seats, Robert!' he moaned, 'You won't be thinking this is "grand" when you get a wooden splinter stuck in your—'

'De Rainault!' shouted the King, cutting off Hugo's profanity-to-be.

'Yes?' said both the Sheriff and Abbot Hugo, almost in unison.

The King swiftly turned his head round, 'I was talking to the Sheriff, not the clergy!' he snapped.

'Sire?' enquired the Sheriff.

'What are we waiting for?' he snarled, 'Let the festivities begin!'

The Sheriff nodded and stood up from his seat in between King John on his left and Abbot Hugo on his right. He raised his arms aloft and shouted loudly, 'Your attention, everyone!'

Gisburne, who was stood by the side of the Royal box, took this as his cue to help out—mainly because nobody seemed to take any notice of the Sheriff's command.

'Attention everyone!' Gisburne bellowed, in the deep, rich voice that seemed impossible to have emanated from his thin frame.

The crowd began to quieten down, though not completely.

'I *demand* your attention!' cried the Sheriff.

'The Sheriff *demands* your attention!' Gisburne shouted, even louder.

'Listen to your Sheriff!' yelled the Sheriff, frustrated that sections of the crowd were still chattering amongst themselves.

'Listen to your Sheriff!' echoed Gisburne, at a higher volume.

'That's enough, Gisburne!' shouted the Sheriff, directing his ire at his deputy.

'That's enough, Gis—' began Gisburne, clearly running on automatic at just the wrong moment.

The crowd, amused by the mistake, began

to laugh and some wondered if it was part of the performance. One villager clapped politely, and then they all joined in.

'Idiots,' the Sheriff muttered, under his breath, but now he knew he had their ears, he began again. 'His Majesty has declared that our evening's festivities—the Mystery Plays, which he has written himself especially for your entertainment—shall now begin!'

A huge cheer arose from the assembly of villagers, with a smattering of more applause, as a tart fanfare played out over their heads and caused them to turn back to the semi-circle of stages.

As soon as the musical motif had finished playing, the actors strode on to the first of the stages, emoting and enunciating for all they were worth.

The first line was delivered on a plate of melodrama with a side helping of stiffness, 'Brave soldier, how goes the battle here in the Holy Land?'

The second actor responded, equally melodramatically and stiffly, pressing the back of his hand to his forehead to feign upset, 'Not well, Commander. Scores of our soldiers have been killed. The infidels storm our gates. Our cause seems lost.'

The crowd jumped as the same blast of fanfare struck up again and assaulted their hearing.

'What ho?' said the first actor, waving his arm dramatically to the side, 'Who is this who now approaches, riding tall, sword brandished in his mighty arms, and shield gleaming as if carrying the light of heaven?'

Another actor stepped on to the stage: the same "hero" whom the King had seen perform in the rehearsals back at the Great Hall in London. His costume was bulked out with padding, worn over an already impressive physique; his cheeks had been painted rouge with the juice of berries. His beard and hair were cut short and styled and his costume shone so brightly white that some of the audience began to shield their eyes.

This actor spoke in a snarling drawl, facing out to the audience even more than his fellow supporting artistes.

'It is I, King John… your leader. And now that I am here, the infidels will cower in fear, run for the hills and our mighty cause will win the day.'

The first actor on the stage almost fainted with the forced excitement he put into his delivery of his follow-up line, 'Oh, fabulous day! Oh, heavenly glory! Was there ever a truer arm, a keener eye and a steelier resolve than that of our King, our magnificent leader?'

CHAPTER TEN

The first play had been epic in itself, but the second play seemed to top it. King John was essentially the bravest of all the heroes ever, and the crowd were—somewhat unexpectedly—lapping it up.

The spectacle of what was being shown, even though it was at times hammy and forced, was winning them over through the sheer power of words and seemingly impossible magical effects. The crowd had gasped at the dragon peeking round from behind one side of the stage, smoke and fire belching out of its nostrils. Its tail swished out from behind the opposite end of the stage, giving the illusion of a long, large reptile; one filled in the body, neck, wings and clawed legs with one's own imagination.

The actor playing King John raised his sword skyward as the crescendo of the finale of this second play was reached, and bravely intoned, 'And though I face this dragon with hornèd head and breath of fire, I know that God is by my side. I shall be resolute and, in the end, victorious.'

'My liege,' said a fellow actor on his knees in awe of this powerful king, 'Your bravery knows not any limit. Is it even possible that you are of mortal flesh and blood? I know of no ordinary man who would undertake to slay this mighty beast.'

The heroic King John turned away from the audience and appeared to stab the backdrop at the back of the stage and, therefore, into the middle of the hidden beast.

'Take that!' he cried out.

There was a loud, mechanical roar that boomed around the clearing and startled the audience.

'And that!' he said, stabbing the backdrop again.

Another mechanical roar sounded out, this time not quite catching the audience so off-guard.

Although not in the script, the actor—caught up in the gasps of shock and excitement from the crowd—couldn't resist ad-libbing one final line and inserting another thrust, which was a surprise to the man creating the roaring of the dragon.

'Die, thy foul beast!' improvised the Player King.

Unfortunately, this time there was nothing but silence. To the audience, it signalled that the beast had been slain, and they began to cheer and applaud. This was a stroke of some luck, as it meant they couldn't hear the swearing from the Master of the Revels, who was the one working the mechanical roar behind the stage… and had narrowly missed being stabbed in the head by the unexpected sword thrust. What was signalled by this sequence of events was equally clear to the Master of the Revels: that the actor on stage was getting far too big for his royal boots.

Unfortunately, the third of the plays, now nearing its climax, wasn't quite as fun or as powerful as the previous two and the audience were starting to become a little restless. It didn't help that it was made up of a series of overly-long soliloquies, most delivered in a depressingly monotone manner.

'*How do I cope with such power, grace and nobility? No mortal man can know the agonies I suffer in the name of my people,*' the actor King John recited.

As the speech droned on further, the Sheriff beckoned Gisburne to come closer to the Royal box and leaned forward. 'Gisburne?'

'Yes, my lord?'

'I have reason to believe that Robin Hood has been spotted a little deeper in Sherwood nearby, gathering his outlaws for an attack on King John.'

'No common man can know how the depth of my love for people leaves little room for anything else. I am alone in my duty, and yet I live for that very same duty.'

'You cannot be serious. Who told you this, my lord?'

'I *am* serious, Gisburne... and do not question my sources, you underling. I know what I'm doing. I want you to gather our men and the King's guard, and take them out into the forest in search of the wolfshead. I want you to head him off before he even reaches these pageant grounds.'

'But the King will be left here unprotected!'

'Do as you're told and stop blathering nonsense. I myself am here protecting His Highness.'

Gisburne tried to disguise what turned out to be a loud and heavy sigh. 'Yes, my lord.'

'For to be a King is second only to that of an angel from heaven. I am both leader and protector and I carry the word of God. God is my companion and advisor.'

Gisburne walked away from the Royal box. 'You there, soldier!' he barked. 'Gather the men; we ride into Sherwood this very moment to apprehend Robin Hood.'

'*Now,* my lord?'

'Yes, you heard me. He's been spotted rounding up his tiny rebel army, and they're on their way here. Now, move!'

'*The wisdom flows from me to my people comes from God. I know that often I demand a great deal from my subjects, but it is not my choice.*'

Little John, stationed close enough to have heard the exchange, turned to find Robin already at his side. 'I assume you heard that? The sheriff is sending his men—and the King's—into Sherwood.'

'Yes, very clever: using us as bait—without realising we're actually here—and clearing this place of any soldiers loyal to King John.'

'...and leaving him unprotected from an attack by De Vesci's soldiers,' said Little John.

Robin nodded, 'Whatever is going to happen, it will happen soon... I'm guessing just as the last play—*The Hell Mouth*—is being presented. Spread the word to the others to get ready, John.'

'Right, will do!' replied Little John, moving off as stealthily as he could.

'For when you represent the Holy Spirit, the divine will, yours is a power that can only bring good to the world, and it cannot be denied, lest the Devil find a small crack through which he can slither...'

The end of the third play had heralded a smattering of applause, but it was clear that—as short as the runtime was for each piece—the audience were tiring and hadn't particularly enjoyed the serious speeches and lack of action in the act that had just finished.

Then, as the actor who had played King John throughout strode onto the platform in front of the giant Devil's Head, there was a frisson of excitement. 'Now,' he began, 'it is my privilege to bring to the stage a very special guest for the finale from our quartet of Mystery Plays. This evening, I have had the great honour of portraying His Majesty King John. Let's hear a cheer for the King...'

'Yay!' shouted a handful of those in the audience, half-heartedly.

'I can't hear you!' said the fake King, knowing how important it was to whip up enthusiasm, and to get the audience back on side for this last—and most impressive—play. 'Now, a *real* cheer for the King, please!'

As he raised his arms, the audience shouted 'Yay!' with a lot more conviction. But it still wasn't enough for the actor on stage.

'If *I* were the King,' he said, 'I'd be disappointed by that. And knowing our King is actually here tonight… I *know* you can do better than that.'

The Master of the Revels, positioned behind the stage and preparing to operate the Devil's Head when it was needed, put his own head in his hands. The adulation from the audience for the character he was playing had gone to the actor's head. The Master prayed that the *real* King wouldn't have *his* head for this… especially as King John had originally requested this particular actor be replaced all those weeks ago during the rehearsals.

'Come on,' said the actor, 'One more time. Let's hear it for *King John!*' He raised his prop sword in the air, puffed out his chest, and was drowned by the volume of a cheer that was not only loud but also long. In the Royal box, the real King John stood up and gave the audience a wave and a small bow.

'For this, our final play, I myself will be leaving the stage,' the actor stated, adding a pause after these words. In his mind, this would elicit a moan of sorrow from the audience, but his expectation failed spectacularly, leaving the pause to feel more uncomfortable. Regaining his composure he continued, 'I know that you will miss me, however you will surely be awed to learn that King John will be appearing *as himself* in *The Hell Mouth!*'

The Sheriff's jaw dropped and he turned to look at the standing figure of his King.

There was a genuine collective intake of breath from the audience, as this was something they had never expected to happen. A nobleman, slumming it on stage, with travelling showmen? And playing himself?

'*What?*' finally uttered the Sheriff.

'Ladies and gentlemen, I give you… His Royal Majesty, King John!'

Caught up in all the excitement, the crowd went a little wild, cheering and chanting the King's name.

Moving to exit the Royal box, the King explained to the Sheriff, 'A little surprise for everyone here, de Rainault!'

'More than a *little* surprise,' the Sheriff muttered, his head swimming as he began to see himself losing control of the plan that he and De Vesci had so carefully put into place.

King John left the box and, stepping through the parting crowd as he made his way towards the stage, shouted back to the Sheriff, 'I shall defeat the Devil, Herne and Robin Hood by my own hand... and this braying rabble shall witness it!'

'But... but...' stuttered the Sheriff, desperately wondering how he could conceivably coax the King back into the place his plan needed him to be.

The King grinned as he walked away, and said, 'This is how you destroy one legend and replace it with a new one!'

CHAPTER ELEVEN

In the climatic scene of *The Hell Mouth*, the sound of real metal swords permeated the still night air, as they clanged together during a fierce fight between the real King John—playing himself—and an actor in black armour, playing a demon. The audience were utterly enraptured and had crowded closer to the stage to witness the culmination of this Easter experience.

'Back, demon; back, I say!' shouted King John, bringing his sword down hard on that of the other actor's. Oddly, even though he'd never before trodden the boards, the King seemed to be somewhat of a natural performer. Rather than the melodramatic and wooden contributions from other actors, there was natural reality to his performance that intrigued the crowd. His rage seemed real, as he continued to deliver his speech, 'Though you have the power of evil to lend weight to your sword and strength to your arm, you cannot triumph over the forces of good...'

The next downward slice of King John's sword brought the demon down onto his knees. His black armour was in fact not made out of metal but was a clever fabric substitute made to look convincing, but was lighter and allowed a greater range of movement, including his current action of throwing his arms up in mercy.

'I, King John, fight you on behalf of my subjects with all the power which God, my saviour and my beacon, has bestowed upon me.' The rage that so entranced the crowd reached a peak with his next line, 'Die, demon! *DIE!*'

King's John thrust his sword to the side of his foe, obviously missing him, but—due to the carefully-calculated angle—it looked to the audience as though the demon had genuinely been run through. The illusion was assisted by the unholy scream that the demon omitted, which was blood-curdling beyond belief.

Shortly after the scream had ended, the sound of artificial thunder rumbled across the audience—

full of drums and acoustic clatter. This signified the Gates of Hell being opened; wafts of smoke and a sickly light were projected from the open jaw of the Devil's Head.

'What be this?' cried King John, in mock horror. 'A conflagration does appear before me; the opening of a fiery portal. It can be nothing other than the entrance to Hell itself!'

From within this entrance came a deep and rich voice, echoing into the forest clearing as if it had travelled up from the underworld. Backstage, Alonzo was speaking into a metal tube that funnelled his voice, distorting it as it travelled through a tapered mouthpiece to its flared exit.

'**King John!**' declared Alonzo, his mysterious and troubling transformed voice floating on the night air like clouds covering the moon. It was definitely unsettling the audience as intended.

'Hark!' cried out King John. 'A voice calls to me from this maelstrom of fire and brimstone!'

'**King John, hear my words!**'

The King played up to the crowd, pulling a worried face at the many that were intently staring back at him with an equally worried expression.

'**It is I, Lucifer, come to ravage your people and bring turmoil and pestilence to your kingdom.**'

'Lucifer? The *Devil?*' uttered a pretending-to-be-shocked King, clearly loving every moment of his time on stage.

'Yes!' said Alonzo's voice, "**the Devil. Yet I go by other names. Some call me *the Horned One*. To others I am *Beelzebub*. Though I am better known amongst *your* subjects as... *Herne the Hunter*.**'

The crowd, not for the first time this evening, gasped at the revelation, which soon was followed by intense murmurings.

'*Herne the Hunter* you say?' repeated King John, driving home the point. 'Why do *you* appear before me? I've conquered your demon. I have cast you out from my lands. I have protected my people. You have no place here.'

The voice of Lucifer continued on, reverberating all around, '**Just as *your* useless God sent his son to do his bidding, so too do *I* have a son, and his job is to fight you at every turn, spreading evil throughout your domain.**'

King John knew the best part was coming. If the audience had been shocked by the announcement of Herne the Hunter being the Devil, then they were going to be amazed at whom this Devil's son was. '*You* have a *son?*' asked a 'shocked' King John, playing to the audience even more. 'By what name is Herne's evil son known?'

'**He is known as...** *Robin Hood!*'

This elicited another audible gasp and further excited murmuring from the assembled audience.

'I shall fight this "Robin Hood" and free my people from his evil grasp!' vowed King John, holding his sword aloft.

Robin and his outlaw band noticed a few cheers amongst the throng, which was somewhat disturbing. The power of the words used, as well as that of the performance and onstage trickery, was beginning to affect the minds of some of the more easily swayed villagers.

Lucifer spoke in angry tones, '**Then I shall curse thee, by setting a horde of demons upon you.**'

'Do your worst,' demanded the King, 'your evil missives cannot stop me!'

This time, there were genuine shrieks of terror dotted around, as two short 'demons' took to the stage. Each was the size of an infant, and moved in a frighteningly jerky way as the strings attached to them were manipulated from above.

'Look, Robin!' shouted Will Scarlet, pointing, 'There's demons! *Real* demons! Dancing an' jiggling on stage!'

Much, in soothing tones, patted Will Scarlet on the back. 'Rest easy, Will,' he said, 'they're just stage illusions.'

Will Scarlet turned to look at Much with a look of pure incredulity on his face. 'When did *you* get to be such an expert, Much?' he snarled. 'They look ruddy real to me!'

'It's a couple of devil doll *puppets,*' explained Much, remembering how he himself had at first been shocked by them when helping Alonzo, 'They're not *real,*' he added, bluntly, as if he were an elder pouring scorn on a youth.

'Hmmm. Devil doll puppets, you say?' pondered Robin.

Back on the stage, the little marionettes did their thing, disturbing the majority of the audience. King John was eager to reach the climax of the play on a high. 'Begone, dancing demons,' he yelled. 'Yield to my mighty sword. I say, be—'

A whistling sound, ending with a resounding thud, disturbed the end of his sentence as an arrow embedded itself into the wooden frame behind him, having narrowly missed his shoulder.

King John was genuinely shocked, 'What? Who fired an arrow at me?' he quivered. The audience believed this latest incident to be part of the plot.

Vaulting deftly up onto the stage, Robin quickly called out, 'Protect the King!' and drew Albion, his sword.

'Go, Robin!' snarled Will Scarlet, shouting across from the other side of the stage to Robin, knowing that his leader was desperate to get to Alonzo quickly, 'We'll protect the King!'

The audience still assumed this was part of the play and began to cheer... until people around them—De Vesci's soldiers—drew their swords. Will Scarlet, Friar Tuck, Little John and Much quickly formed something of a guard of honour around the front of the stage and prepared to face the oncoming assault. Soon, with the sounds of swords clashing and the swish of Little John's quarterstaff connecting with advancing bodies, a majority of the audience began to panic.

Robin darted through the opening of the Devil's Head into the black space inside, and saw Alonzo with his metal Lucifer voice-maker stand up in confused shock. 'What is going on out there?' he asked, genuinely confused.

Nasir, who had leapt on to the stage to shield the King, a sword in each hand, caught sight of his friend unsheathing his weapon through the open mouth. 'Alonzo!' he shouted, sharply.

'Don't move,' ordered Robin, using his sword to knock the metal device out of Alonzo's grasp, 'or you will meet Lucifer soon enough!'

Alonzo stayed surprisingly calm, 'I don't know what madness this is,' he said in a low rumble as he reached for his hilt, 'but when a man draws a sword on me, I am compelled to engage him. En garde!'

Both swords quickly met and there was a flurry of movement as neither man gave an inch to the other. The fighting was ferocious and quick. With a swirl of his flowing, ornate clothing, Alonzo spun away from a particularly vicious swipe by Robin and ended up the other side of him. Robin turned quickly to counteract the expected return thrust but slipped on the smooth wood underfoot, though he was steadied by his frame landing up against the back portion of the Hell Mouth construction.

Alonzo, now with his back to the stage and stood in the entrance of the Devil's Head's mouth, was blocking Robin's escape route. He smiled at his opponent, not menacingly but warmly. 'You're good, my young buck, I'll give you that,' he said, passing his sword back and forth between his hands with a little flourish. 'But my years of experience as a warrior give me the edge over your energised bravado. I will feel extremely sad to end you.'

Yet as the word 'bravado' left his lips, he felt something cold and thin at his throat.

'Stop right there, my friend,' Nasir whispered into Alonzo's ear, having crept up behind him from the main stage.

'Nasir?' Alonzo sighed, questioningly, 'You would hold a knife to my throat? What have I done to warrant such betrayal?'

'You have threatened my leader. This I cannot allow. My loyalty lies with Robin Hood.'

'What?' said Alonzo, 'I think you'll find *he* threatened *me* first!'

'I have come to stop you from killing the King,' Robin stated, relieved by Nasir's stealthy and timely intervention.

Alonzo frowned, 'Killing the... what are you talking about? Are you mad?'

Nasir lightened the heavy pressing of his knife on his friend's throat. 'You are not part of a plot to assassinate the King?' he asked.

There was a single burst of a laugh from Alonzo, 'Me? Certainly not!'

'Do you believe him, Nasir?' asked Robin, still ready with Albion should the fight continue.

Nasir paused, as if mulling it over. Through the Hell Mouth came the noise of sword-fighting outside of this darkened enclave, alongside panicked shouts and screams from audience members unsure whether to disperse and risk being felled by other soldiers that might be on hand, or to stay where they were and watch the spectacle of King John being defended by Robin Hood's band of outlaws.

There was a hypnotic calmness to Alonzo's next uttering. 'I swear upon my sword, Nasir,' he said, urgently, 'upon my sword.'

It was a phrase that Nasir had heard before, flashing him back to fighting side-by-side overseas, when they were younger and more hot-headed.

Nasir nodded, removing the knife from Alonzo's throat and stated, 'I believe him.'

'Thank you,' Alonzo replied, 'I could no more kill the King than chop off my own hand.'

Robin, now knowing how loyal Nasir was—and how he expected that same loyalty from others—realised that Alonzo was innocent of what they had suspected. 'Then keep your hand and help us fight off his attackers,' he urged, smiling at the Moor.

Having secured away his knife, Nasir removed his two swords from the crossing of sheaths that adorned his back, ready to return to the fray. 'You wanted one more cause worth fighting for?' he said to Alonzo 'Surely now you have it!'

'I do, my brother-in-arms, I do. Like old times, eh?'

Emerging from the relative cocoon of silence that was the inside of the Devil's Head, the two warrior brothers and Robin came back out onto the stage and were met instantly by a scene of carnage, sweat and death. Will Scarlet spotted them just as the butt of his sword connected with the face of a soldier; the reappearance of his leader alongside the satisfying sound of the crunching of nose cartilage making him smile.

'Robin! Nasir! 'Appy you could find the time to join us!' he said. 'Though John, Tuck, Much an' I 'ave barely broken a sweat fighting off these blockheads!' he added, sarcastically.

Behind the stage of the Hell Mouth, Marion was becoming frustrated with her job of standing with the horses, when she would normally be stood shoulder-to-shoulder with her friends in the thick of the fighting. Even after all their time together in which she had proven her worth, Robin still often treated her like the lady she didn't want to be anymore and would try to keep her safe rather than keep her alongside him. She knew why he did it—and she loved him for it in one way—but she hadn't joined his noble cause, believing in his passion to challenge injustice, to be stood kicking her heels behind a massive wooden stage; to be sectioned off from the action that was so noisily taking place in front of it.

It was then that she was shocked to see King John fall out of a small, well-hidden slit that constituted the exit from inside the Devil's Head where Robin, Nasir and Alonzo had faced off. As they had returned to the stage to join the fighting, they had not noticed that the King, protected by outlaws on stage whom he'd happily see hang, crawl into the Hell Mouth to search for an escape. Cowardly belying the character he had portrayed on stage—who had been full of swagger and rage and strength—the King screamed almost like a baby when he saw Marion.

'Help!' he cried, 'I must escape!'

Marion stood firm, both her hands holding the reins of several now panicked horses, 'Not yet, Your Highness. Wait for Robin Hood; he'll protect you.'

But, as she said that, she was shoved angrily to the side by the furious and frightened King. 'Out of my way, stupid woman!' he snapped, as Marion fell to the ground heavily. As she did so, she tried not to let go of the horses and, still holding their reins, twisted awkwardly, causing her to hit the side of her head on the hard floor.

'Robin Hood is clearly here to kill me!' continued King John, 'I am the victim of a most vicious plot!'

He clambered unsteadily onto the back of one of the horses to which Marion had been tending, yanking on the reins as he tore them from her grasp.

Dazed, Marion shook her head as King John galloped off into the forest behind her, and her vision swam. She swore she saw a tiny figure dart across from the exit, make its way to another horse, and acrobatically leap into the saddle. She felt another set of reins released from her grasp unexpectedly, as she struggled to hold on to the others from her prone position, the horses now extremely jittery.

As the second horse disappeared into the trees, manic, high-pitched, childish peals of laughter seemed to hang in the night air.

CHAPTER TWELVE

It had been obvious from the start that the outlaws were outnumbered, but this had never stopped them before in a skirmish, and they had the guile and gumption to play to their strengths, supporting each other in a way that a non-cohesive phalanx of soldiers failed to achieve.

However, with nowhere to escape other than into the Hell Mouth, the onslaught was unremitting. No sooner had they felled one set of soldiers from their superior position on the stage, than another set of attackers would take the place of the fallen foes.

As the outlaws' opponents were not dressed as soldiers – having needed to blend in with the audience as part of the assassination plot – things were made even more difficult; care had to be taken not to mistake a panicking villager for an attacking soldier as the now-fleeing audience had decided that enough was enough.

Little John shouted over to Robin, 'We can't hold them all off forever! What should we do?'

'We can only do our best, John!' shouted back Robin. As he did so, and looked across to Little John, he realised that the place where the King had been cowering was now vacant of a Royal presence. 'Where's the King?' he yelled.

'He's gone!' replied a shocked Little John, glancing behind him.

'I have to find him,' said Robin. 'Even though we're protecting him from De Vesci's men, he's still in great danger.'

'But the Moor fights with us. He's no assassin!' answered Little John.

'I know. Yet I suspect the King's life is in danger from *another*. I believe there is still an assassin on the loose.'

'Who could it be, though?' asked Little John, as he spun around to fell an approaching soldier with a hefty swipe of his giant quarterstaff. But, as he turned back to hear Robin's answer, he saw that Robin was gone too.

'Robin?' he cried out, *'Robin?'*

Robin slipped out of the exit in the back of the Hell Mouth and bounded over to where Marion was sitting on the ground, cradling her head. He almost shocked her as he grasped her arm and helped her to her feet.

'Marion!' he exclaimed, 'Are you hurt?'

Marion still felt groggy, but her vision had returned to normal and she knew that, aside from a developing lump under her hair, it could have been worse—especially with the horses trampling and rearing up around her.

'I'm... I'm fine!' she muttered, and then suddenly spoke faster, worriedly, 'Robin, the King took off on horseback. And moments later, I think someone went after him. In the dark, I couldn't tell who it was, I'm sorry. I assume it was the assassin.'

'Yes, I suspect so. And I *think* I know who that assassin might be.'

Robin climbed up into the saddle of one of the remaining horses.

'If you're leaving, I'm going to help the others!' Marion said, feeling more brave than her headache wanted her to be.

'No, you should stay here!' said Robin, turning the horse's head in the direction of Sherwood.

But Marion had already picked up her bow and arrows from where she had stashed them and was heading towards the Hell Mouth. 'I must stand by them!' she said, itching to be in the thick of the battle rather than be sidelined for any longer.

Robin grinned, loving her spirit and regretting his instinct for overprotection, knowing that Marion could fend for herself better than he could protect her.

'Then fight well, my love,' he exclaimed, as the horse broke into a gallop, 'I must rescue the King.'

Standing back-to-back, Nasir and Alonzo were still fighting off swathes of attackers, as they rotated like clockwork when another soldier appeared before either of them.

'This brings back memories; eh, Nasir?'

'Very much, my friend.'

A quick thrust and parry and two more soldiers were dispatched. They were like a well-oiled fighting machine, linked together in movement and mind.

Suddenly though, Alonzo cried out in pain. He doubled over and clutched his stomach. 'No! My pain returns,' he cried in panic, knowing that he needed the contents of the green bottle that would be out of his reach unless someone could run backstage for it. 'No! Not now,' he roared, his knees weakening. He was about to implore Nasir to help him when another soldier appeared, witnessing his ailing stance.

'You are ill, Moor?' he sneered mockingly. 'I have a cure for you. Take this, you worthless savage!'

Alonzo cried out as the soldier's sword entered his flesh and felled him.

'No!' shouted Nasir, swinging round after finishing off another soldier on his side, catching his friend as he fell. The soldier who had stabbed Alonzo was briefly surprised to note that he'd been stabbed too; Nasir had slashed out with one arm at the same time as he had caught a collapsing Alonzo with the other. The surprise lasted only until the soldier's death, which came before he hit the ground.

'My friend, your wound...'

'Deep and fatal, Nasir,' Alonzo replied, in agony. 'I asked Allah for one last battle,' he said weakly, 'and I give thanks to Him for granting my wish.'

'One should be careful what one wishes for,'

Nasir muttered, and Alonzo grinned, regardless of whether it had been meant in humour or sadness.

'The King is gone!' noted one of the advancing soldiers; the others so far had been too busy engaging in battle to look properly around the stage onto which they were climbing.

'Retreat!' shouted another, not wishing to die by the skilled hands of the outlaws... though he was too late, as an arrow loosed by Marion from the arching frame of the Hell Mouth found its intended target. The soldier fell backwards off the stage and into the crowd.

'De Vesci's men are running,' sneered Will Scarlet, wiping away the sweaty fringe from his eyes.

Little John, leaning heavily on his quarterstaff as he caught his breath, replied, 'They were here to kill the King, not die by our swords. And they've failed in their task.'

'There's no point in them staying in Nottingham now,' proclaimed Marion, letting fly with another arrow that found its mark. 'I might as well give them something to leave with,' she added, annoyed she'd missed the main fight.

Friar Tick, able to drop his sword to the floor from his right hand now nursed a thin cut to his left arm. More than relieved, he was completely spent of energy and had expected the next wave of soldiers to be the one that downed him. 'I'm sure even De Vesci is well on his way back north,' he panted, with extreme fatigue.

Edward of Wickham, who had fought to get to the front of the crowd in order to assist the outlaws who regularly helped out his village, was still a few rows back. Yet he was able to calm the then-still-agitated audience by shouting out, 'The outlaws have protected the King! All hail Robin Hood!'

This was enough for the crowd to realise they were safe again, and there was a muted cheer that rose up further as a wave of relief washed over them all.

'All hail Robin Hood's men!' shouted Edward, and the cheer grew louder.

The Sheriff, still sitting uncomfortably in the Royal box, yelled at the retreating soldiers as they passed him by. 'Stop them, you mindless morons,' he shouted, 'Robin Hood isn't even *with* them. Stop the outlaws!'

Abbot Hugo, having kept a keen eye over what had transpired, was already getting up to leave. 'Save your voice, Robert. It seems all your soldiers have departed and the crowd is firmly on the outlaw's side,' he said. 'You're helpless, unless you wish to follow the Hooded Man into the Hell Mouth and fight the wolfshead by yourself?'

The Sheriff gave out a resigned sigh, 'No, Hugo, I don't,' he snapped. 'After tonight's debacle, I would rather go back to my castle and empty a huge cask of wine.'

'You're not worried about the King?' Abbot Hugo asked, raising an eyebrow.

'He'll have to wrestle with his own demons,' muttered the Sheriff, 'There's nothing I can do for him now.'

Much, frantic about what to do, had dragged Marion to Alonzo's side, hoping her skills at mending them could be used to help save his foreign friend. 'Alonzo, you're hurt! I've brought Marion to you. She'll know what to do. Nasir, he's going to be okay, right?' he babbled, kneeling down near the dying Moor.

'I am afraid not,' Nasir whispered, saddened.

Marion had removed Alonzo's hand from his stomach and took one sad look at the wound the soldier had inflicted. She shook her head. 'There's nothing I can do for you.'

'I know,' said Alonzo, weakly, and then turned his attention to Much, who was starting to sob.

'It is all right, Much,' he soothed, his voice still deep but with the strength sucked out of it. 'This is exactly how I wanted to die—in the heat of a battle for a worthy cause, surrounded by good friends.'

'No,' cried Much, 'It's not *fair!*'

Alonzo struggled to raise himself a little, helped by Marion, 'Much, will you please do me one favour?' he asked.

'Anything,' answered Much, through his tears.

'Look after my brother Nasir. He is a clumsy bungler when it comes to handling a sword. He needs somebody brave and clever like you to protect him.'

Nasir smiled.

Much took the request in earnest. 'I— I promise.'

Alonzo fell backwards, the weight of his frame meaning Marion could hold him up no longer. Nasir cradled Alonzo's head as the light in his eyes began to fade.

'As for you, dearest Nasir Malik Kemal Inal Ibrahim Shams ad-Dualla Wattab ibn Mahmud,' he whispered.

'Yes?'

'*As-salamu alaykum*, my brother in arms.'

Nasir replied, in kind, '*Wa alaykumu as-salam*, Alonzo da Pian del Carpine.'

This Arabic greeting of 'Peace be unto you'— and its response 'Peace be with you also'—enabled Alonzo to step calmly beyond the realm of the living as he closed his eyes and expired.

CHAPTER THIRTEEN

As the trees of Sherwood flashed by in a blur, King John struggled to hold onto the reins of his fast-paced mount; he was in considerable pain as he bounced ungainly in the saddle.

'Slow down, you stupid nag!' the King yelled at the animal. 'I'm losing my balaaaaaaa—'

The King toppled from his galloping horse and, luckily for him, landed in a thicket at the side of the track. It cushioned his fall and, although the wind was temporarily knocked out of him, it was a far better result than had he not landed on something so relatively soft.

The horse was fast disappearing, stampeding riderless and deeper into Sherwood as the King hauled himself out of the undergrowth and brushed himself down. Flustered, he shouted after his wild steed, 'You filthy beast! I'll have you caught, filleted and served to my army!'

Not used to being alone and unable to call on servants or soldiers, the King found his current situation quite the unsettling experience. At first, the cool darkness of Sherwood was inviting and peaceful, but as he began to pick up the sounds of the forest more clearly, he became increasingly nervous.

An owl hooted almost directly overhead.

'Argh! What was that?' gasped King John, stopping in his tracks and looking around.

A wolf howled in the not-too-far distance, causing the King to gasp again. He stumbled forward, and what had begun a minute or two ago as a leisurely stroll became stutteringly speedy.

Soon, above the calls of the various animals, he heard the approaching thud of a horse's hooves.

'Hello?' he ventured, looking all around him, peering deep into the gloom.

Soon the sound of the hooves stopped and he heard the distinct noise of feet landing on the ground, as someone disembarked. 'Who goes there?' he questioned, his stuttering walk now almost turning into a run.

But there was no reply, only the sounds of Sherwood Forest.

King John stopped and decided to stand his ground. He had no idea to where he was running, and he feared stumbling off the track and into the forest proper; at least he had the advantage of being able to see a person—or an animal—in the moonlight if he stayed out in the open. Yet in this instance he saw no one.

'I am *not* afraid!' snarled the King, his tone proving to anyone or anything that could hear him the exact opposite.

Suddenly there was a high-pitched peal of laughter that sounded like a child had been force-fed Scathlock's ale and then told the funniest joke in the world. The bushes nearby rustled as something that wasn't the breeze moved through them, then a figure emerged onto the track in front of the King.

'God help me!' cried the royal, recoiling backwards at the sight of one of the Devil marionettes that he had previously seen dancing on the stage during *The Hell Mouth*.

Yet this one had no strings attached.

'It's a real demon imp, come to life to torment me! Argh! *Help!*'

The puppet produced a small dirk from his belt and flourished it, all the while jerkily jigging on the forest track, hugely unsettling the King who almost tripped over his own robes as he stumbled backwards, away from the advancing abomination.

'Stop! *Stop!*' shouted the King, before looking first down at the ground and then up at the sky. 'Oh, God! Oh, Satan! I know I've been a foolish, selfish monarch. I've been a wicked man! But if you spare my life, I promise I'll repent!' he pleaded, desperate for the apparition before his eyes to vanish in a puff of smoke.

King John held out a hand, in the hope that his royal position might still hold some sway here on this lonely track in the darkening night. 'Stay back in the name of the King! No... Stop! I'll repent! Please don't kill me. I'll be good to my subjects from now on, I promise! I'll be—'

All this while, the Devil doll had danced its jerking ballet ever closer to the King. Now—issuing an ear-splitting, high-pitched squeal—it lunged at its target with the dagger's glinting razor-sharp point. As it did so, the King raised his hands over his face in fear and fell backwards to the floor.

Just as the doll advanced close enough to strike at the now prone King, the familiar swish of an arrow making its way through the air was heard, following by a grizzly thud as it connected with the Devil doll's head—right between its painted-on eyes. A scream of agony gurgled away as quickly as it had begun; the dance of the Devil doll ceased as its body became as lifeless as the marionette for which the King had mistaken it.

'What? How can it be dead? Does the Devil die from an arrow to the head?' burbled the King, crawling towards the prone body.

Further up the embankment looking over the track, a figure stepped out from the shadows of the trees. The Hooded Man.

'That was no Devil, King John,' said Robin Hood, matter-of-factly.

The King, scrambling to his feet, grimaced when he saw the athletic figure of Robin of Loxley in such a commanding position, bow still in his hand. 'I know what I saw,' he snarled. 'Perhaps it was *you* who bewitched the puppet?' he added, his face gaining back some colour as the shock subsided.

'It was no devil, it was an assassin hired to kill you,' confirmed Robin.

'Hired to kill me?' snapped the King. 'By whom?'

'That's for me to know, and for you to find out!' smiled Robin, 'Let's just say that you need to watch your back among your supposed friends. You may think you have their support but... the Devil is, quite literally, in the detail!'

If the King could have shaken a fist at Robin without it looking like an angry cliché, he would have done. 'Why, you impertinent—' he began, but was interrupted by Robin as the sound of a group of galloping horses snaked through the trees.

'I believe that is your soldiers approaching. You might want to call out and ask them for ride back to Nottingham. Oh, and be sure to tell them that while they were enjoying an evening sojourn in Sherwood Forest looking for Robin Hood, your life was in fact saved by the very same! Farewell, Your Highness!' Robin chided, before disappearing back into the foliage.

King John tried to scramble up the hilly side of the track but ended up simply sliding back down again, chunks of grass and clod in his hands from where he'd tried to hang on. 'Come back here, outlaw; come back here!'

As his feet touched the track again, he shouted out: 'Help! Heeeeellllp!'

As predicted by Robin, the group of soldiers appeared on the track, with Gisburne—atop his usual black stallion—leading them.

'Your Highness, what are you doing in Sherwood?' asked a very surprised Sir Guy.

'Gisburne, you FOOL!' thundered the King. 'I ought to have your *head* for abandoning me,' he bellowed.

'But, my liege,' countered Gisburne, 'I was only following the Sheriff's orders.'

The King fumed and sputtered, 'Then I might just have *his* head too!'

Gisburne offered a hand so that the King could climb up and sit on his horse behind him, though this did not stop the King from shouting, his face as red as a beetroot. Having seated himself in the saddle behind Gisburne, he turned to address the entire group of men. 'You incompetent nincompoops,' he yelled, 'you blithering *IDIOTS!*'

EPILOGUE

The chill had now settled into Sherwood, as it normally did as the evening wore on. There was precious little space between Robin, Marion, Little John, Friar Tuck and Will Scarlet as they huddled together around a roaring fire set in a rough stone circle that kept the flames and heat from reaching further out into the forest itself.

Will Scarlet pondered before spouting a question that sounded like an accusation due to his blunt way of speaking. 'How did you know the assassin was a dwarf disguised as one of Alonzo's Devil dolls, then?'

Robin, warming his hands as the fire crackled, spoke softly. 'It was the phrase you told me Alonzo had shouted when you first encountered him in Sherwood. You were stabbed in the leg by something you thought was a dog, and Alonzo shouted the phrase "Bambola del Diavolo! Salire a bordo!"—I mean, you didn't repeat it *exactly* like that, but Friar Tuck got the gist.'

'Tuck?' queried Will Scarlet.

'Yes, me!' said the jolly Friar. 'I know a smattering of Italian; Robin asked me what it meant, and I translated as best I could. "Bambola del Diavolo" means "Devil doll". Alonzo was telling him to get back in the wagon!'

'And when Much told us he thought he saw one of the devil dolls move its eyes,' added Robin, 'I put it all together.'

'Ahhh, I see now,' said Will Scarlet.

'Yes, though it wasn't until we found out Alonzo *wasn't* the assassin that I knew for certain who the Devil doll had to be.'

'But why did Alonzo bring him here?' asked Marion, lifting her head gently off Robin's shoulder, where she'd been resting it, 'And why was he disguised as the Devil in the first place?'

Little John, now putting the pieces together himself, decided to jump in. 'Alonzo said he had a "big surprise" for the end of *The Hell Mouth*. He said that the crowd would believe the Devil had come to life.'

'Yes, John!' said Robin, 'What better way than to have, at the play's climax, one of the marionette puppets take on a life of its own, suddenly free itself from its strings and prance across the stage?'

'The Devil doll truly come to life!' said Friar Tuck, 'That *would* have been an unforgettable sight.'

'Exactly,' said Robin. 'With the audience under the spell of these plays, it would have utterly shocked all those watching! But under no circumstances could anyone know that Alonzo was travelling with a dwarf; it would have spoiled the illusion.'

Friar Tuck nodded, in agreement. 'It's a magician's rule. You never reveal your secrets.'

'Do you think Alonzo knew that the dwarf planned to kill the King?' asked Marion.

'No, Marion, I think that was a secret the "doll" kept to himself, it's certainly not something he would have felt safe divulging to Alonzo.'

'Hah, yeah,' said Will Scarlet, enacting a passable impression of a Devil doll, with jerky movements and a high-pitched voice, 'Hey, Alonzo! Listen, I'm an assassin hired by the northern barons, and it's my mission to kill the King. But you ain't to tell anyone, right?'

This caused a great deal of laughter around the flickering flames.

'It's quite the plot,' said Little John. 'But even though this particular plan was thwarted, what do you think will happen next? Clearly, there's unrest.'

'King John isn't well liked,' said Friar Tuck. 'I think we all knew that before he was crowned. As a Prince, he was known to be mean-spirited and full of rage.'

'He may well face an outright rebellion someday soon,' said Robin, 'not that *I'm* going to start it!'

'Yes,' said Friar Tuck. 'Such concerns are his problem, not ours. Not right now, anyway.'

'Well,' said Little John, clapping a large hand onto Friar Tuck's shoulder and making him jump, 'I don't know about the rest of you, but all that fighting has made me hungry.'

'Me too!' added Will Scarlet, 'How's about we get Tuck 'ere to cook up that shank of lamb we confiscated from the festivities and have our own well-earned feast?'

'In honour of our brave King, I assume?' chuckled Friar Tuck, shifting his weight to get up.

'Aye, I'll happily join you in cooking the lamb. After all, I'm a growing lad and I need me fill,' joked Little John, who was able to get up quicker than the Friar, before helping him stand with a well-placed hand under his armpit.

Will Scarlet stood up too. 'Long live King John,' he mockingly cheered.

'What *you* getting up for?' asked Little John.

'Coming to 'elp, ain't I?' said Will Scarlet, 'I don't want you scoffing the lot before we've had our turn to taste some!'

'Long live King John indeed,' said Friar Tuck, smiling away as he ambled off to fetch the lamb shank, '...until they try to assassinate him, ideally somewhere far away from us. We certainly don't want the blame!'

'Aye,' said Little John, 'May they have better luck next time!'

The trio of outlaws left the fireside, laughing between themselves, as Robin and Marion stayed to gaze at the flickering patterns that the flames made.

'Robin?' said Marion, after a minute or so, breaking his glassy-eyed concentration.

'Yes, my love?'

'I hope you now know for sure that Nasir is loyal to you, no matter what?'

'I do,' replied Robin. 'Truth be told, I feel foolish for ever doubting him.'

Marion was quick to put things into context. 'He follows you—as do we all—because *you* are the chosen son of Herne. *You* are the one who can best guide us through these dark times into a new age of equality and enlightenment.'

'Thank you, Marion,' nodded Robin, humbled by her turn of phrase and sentiment. 'I will always do my best to live up to your faith in me.'

There was another slight pause as the fire drew them in again.

'By the way,' muttered Robin, half-glancing at Marion, 'where *is* Nasir? And Much, for that matter?'

'They went to the lake, as Nasir wanted to fire a flaming arrow on behalf of Alonzo.'

'So must it be.'

The twang of bowstrings at the edge of the lake could be heard across from the other side as two arrows—both with flaming tips—were consecutively fired. They flew high into the air before their arching descent created a small splash and a loud hiss as each plunged into the water.

'Nasir,' whispered Much, 'do you think Alonzo's spirit will remain here with us in Sherwood?'

'It is possible,' answered Nasir, equally quietly, as a mark of respect. 'He was someone who chose to be in the company of good men who fought for a noble cause.'

Much suddenly pointed across the lake as a figure stood on the other side, the horned headdress creating a silhouette that was easy to identify. 'Look,' he urged Nasir, 'over there, across the lake. It's Herne!'

Both men instantly got down on their knees and bowed their heads.

'Herne protect us!' they mumbled, almost simultaneously.

When they looked up, the form of Herne had vanished. In his place, a rolling mist was making its way across the lake towards them.

'Why do you think Herne came here tonight?' asked Much, getting up and turning to walk back to camp.

'I am certain he has come to welcome the spirit of my brother Alonzo to Sherwood Forest,' stated Nasir as he slowly followed Much, though he took one final look back across the lake now blanketed in the mystical fog, 'Alonzo the Moor is now a part of our legend.'

As the tendrils of mist reached their side of the water, and Much and Nasir left the lake behind, on the chilly wind came the faintest utterance of what could be mistaken for the smallest snippet of a rich, booming laugh.

And then it was gone.

Also from Chinbeard and Oak Tree Books

Richard Carpenter's
ROBIN OF SHERWOOD

THE SCATHLOCK
WOMAN

Jennifer Ash

www.ingramcontent.com/pod-product-compliance
Lightning Source LLC
Chambersburg PA
CBHW011511170626
46810CB00009B/3317